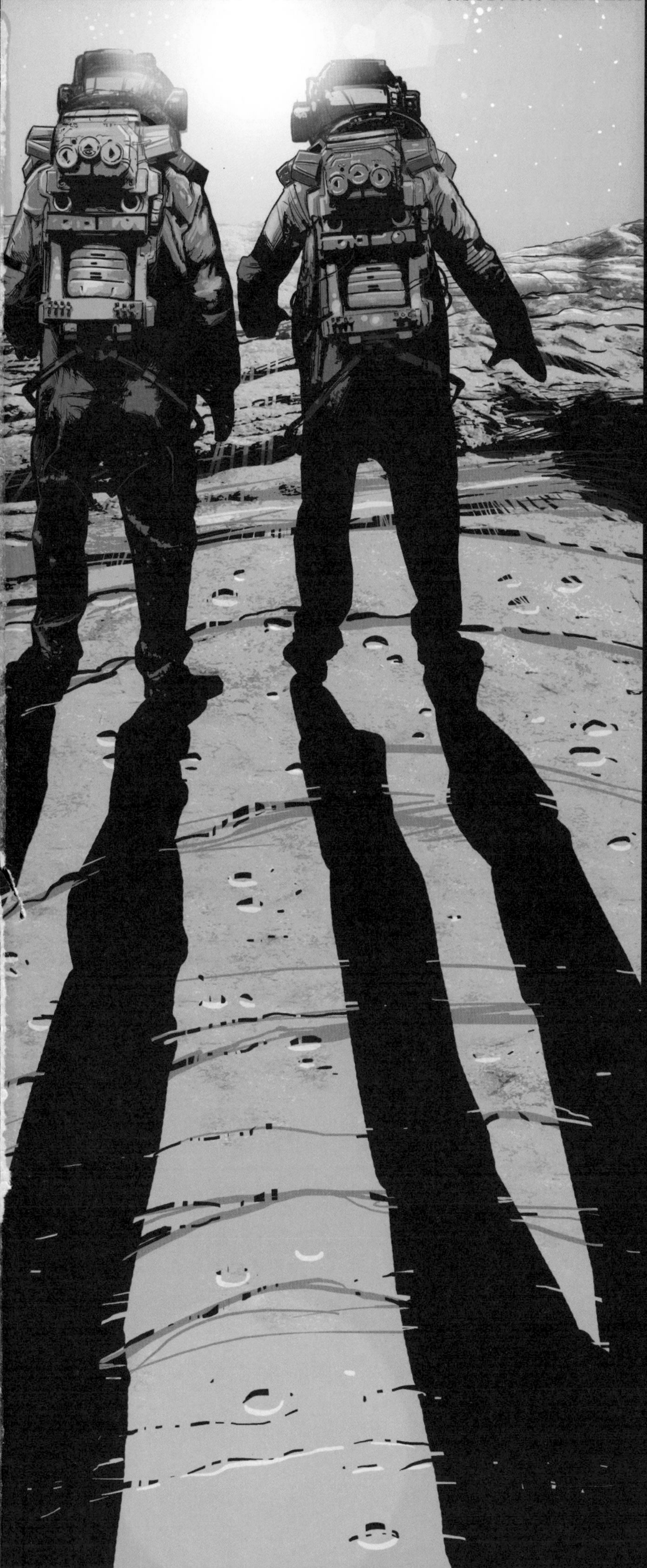

THE CHIMPANZEE COMPLEX

1-PARADOX

SCRIPT: RICHARD MARAZANO
DRAWING: JEAN-MICHEL PONZIO

"Everywhere man feels the terror of mystery and looks up at heaven only with frightened eyes."

Baudelaire, *The Flowers of Evil, (Transl. William Aggeler, 1954)*

CINEBOOK
The 9th Art Publisher

Original title: Le complexe du chimpanzé - Paradoxe

Original edition: © Dargaud Paris, 2007 by Marazano & Ponzio
www.dargaud.com
All rights reserved

English translation: © 2009 Cinebook Ltd

Translator: Jerome Saincantin
Lettering and text layout: Imadjinn
Printed in Spain by Just Colour Graphic

This edition first published in Great Britain in 2009 by
Cinebook Ltd
56 Beech Avenue
Canterbury, Kent
CT4 7TA
www.cinebook.com

A CIP catalogue record for this book
is available from the British Library

ISBN 978-1-84918-002-3

9th CINEBOOK
The 9th Art Publisher

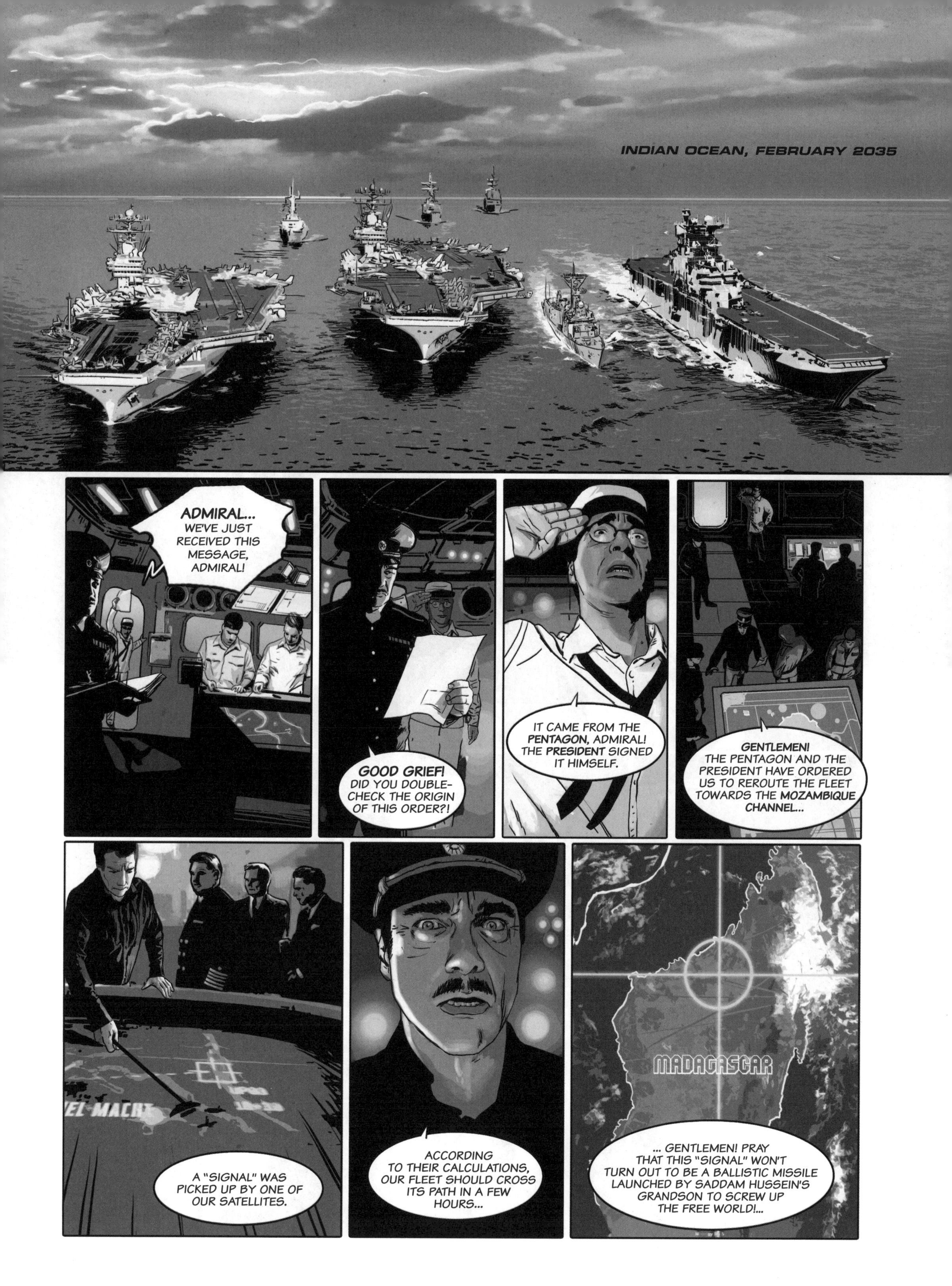
INDIAN OCEAN, FEBRUARY 2035
ADMIRAL... WE'VE JUST RECEIVED THIS MESSAGE, ADMIRAL!
GOOD GRIEF! DID YOU DOUBLE-CHECK THE ORIGIN OF THIS ORDER?!
IT CAME FROM THE PENTAGON, ADMIRAL! THE PRESIDENT SIGNED IT HIMSELF.
GENTLEMEN! THE PENTAGON AND THE PRESIDENT HAVE ORDERED US TO REROUTE THE FLEET TOWARDS THE MOZAMBIQUE CHANNEL...
A "SIGNAL" WAS PICKED UP BY ONE OF OUR SATELLITES.
ACCORDING TO THEIR CALCULATIONS, OUR FLEET SHOULD CROSS ITS PATH IN A FEW HOURS...
MADAGASCAR
... GENTLEMEN! PRAY THAT THIS "SIGNAL" WON'T TURN OUT TO BE A BALLISTIC MISSILE LAUNCHED BY SADDAM HUSSEIN'S GRANDSON TO SCREW UP THE FREE WORLD!...

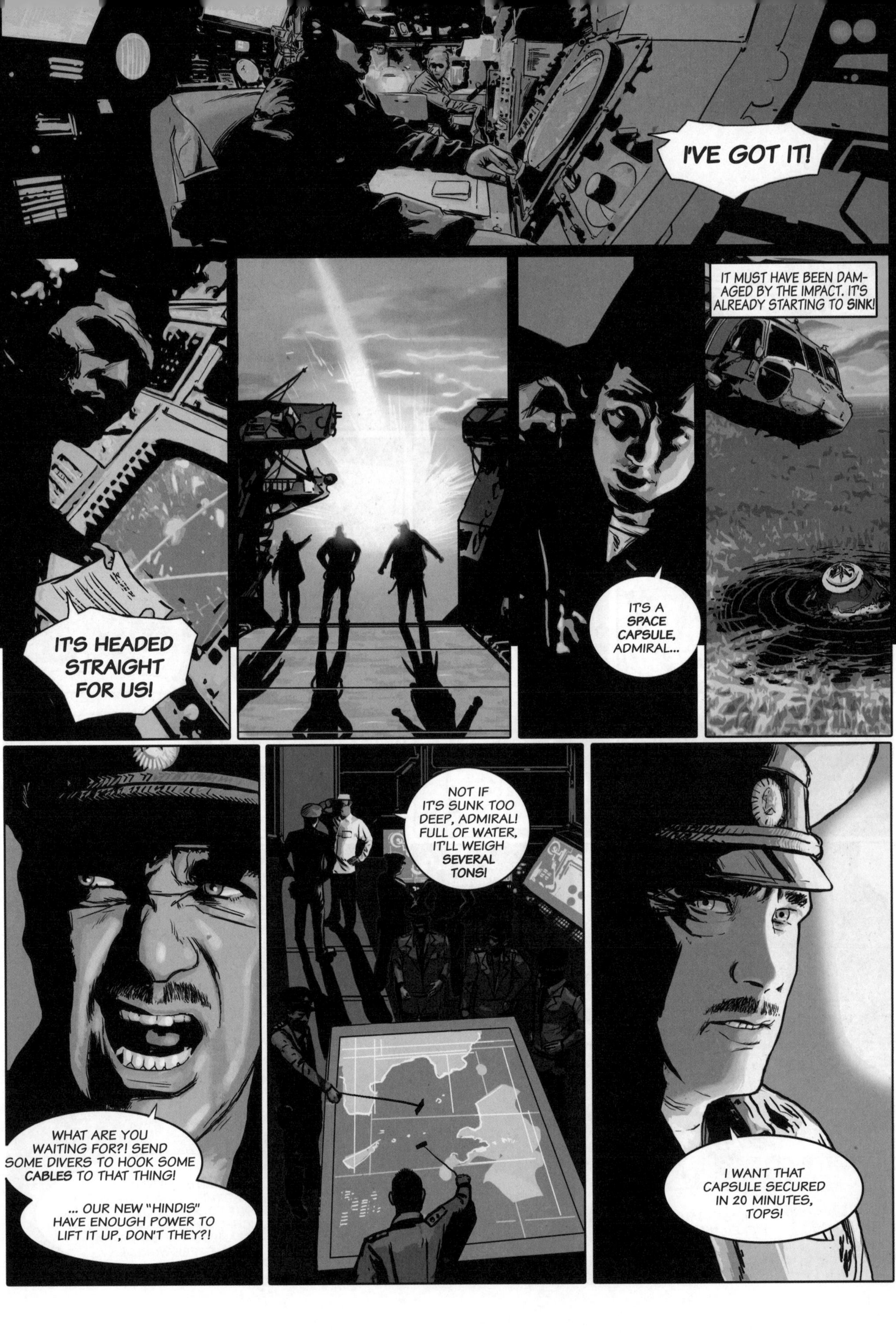
I'VE GOT IT!
IT'S HEADED STRAIGHT FOR US!
IT'S A SPACE CAPSULE, ADMIRAL...
IT MUST HAVE BEEN DAMAGED BY THE IMPACT. IT'S ALREADY STARTING TO SINK!
WHAT ARE YOU WAITING FOR?! SEND SOME DIVERS TO HOOK SOME CABLES TO THAT THING!
... OUR NEW "HINDIS" HAVE ENOUGH POWER TO LIFT IT UP, DON'T THEY?!
NOT IF IT'S SUNK TOO DEEP, ADMIRAL! FULL OF WATER, IT'LL WEIGH SEVERAL TONS!
I WANT THAT CAPSULE SECURED IN 20 MINUTES, TOPS!

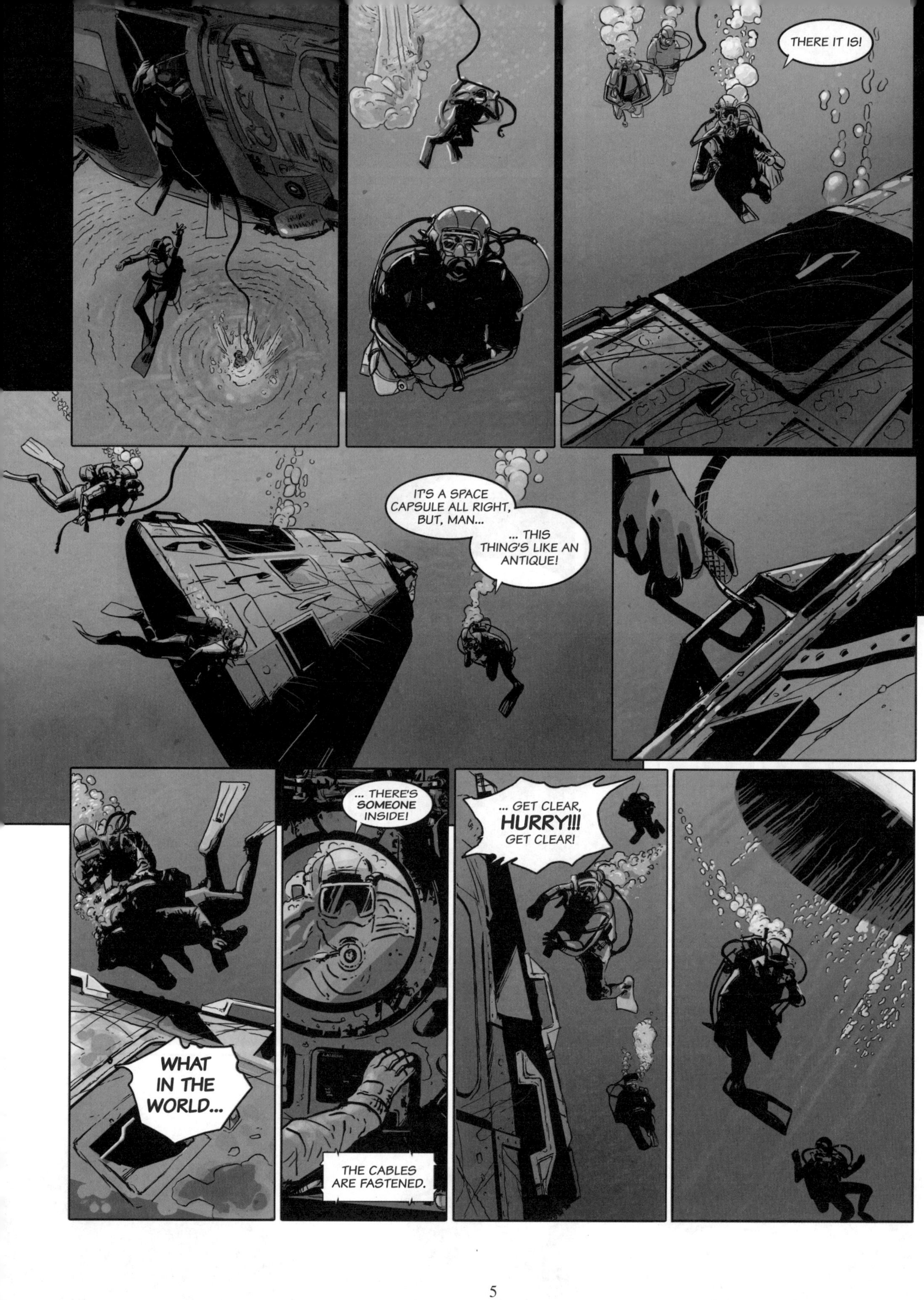
THERE IT IS!
IT'S A SPACE CAPSULE ALL RIGHT, BUT, MAN...
... THIS THING'S LIKE AN ANTIQUE!
WHAT IN THE WORLD...
... THERE'S SOMEONE INSIDE!
THE CABLES ARE FASTENED.
... GET CLEAR, HURRY!!! GET CLEAR!

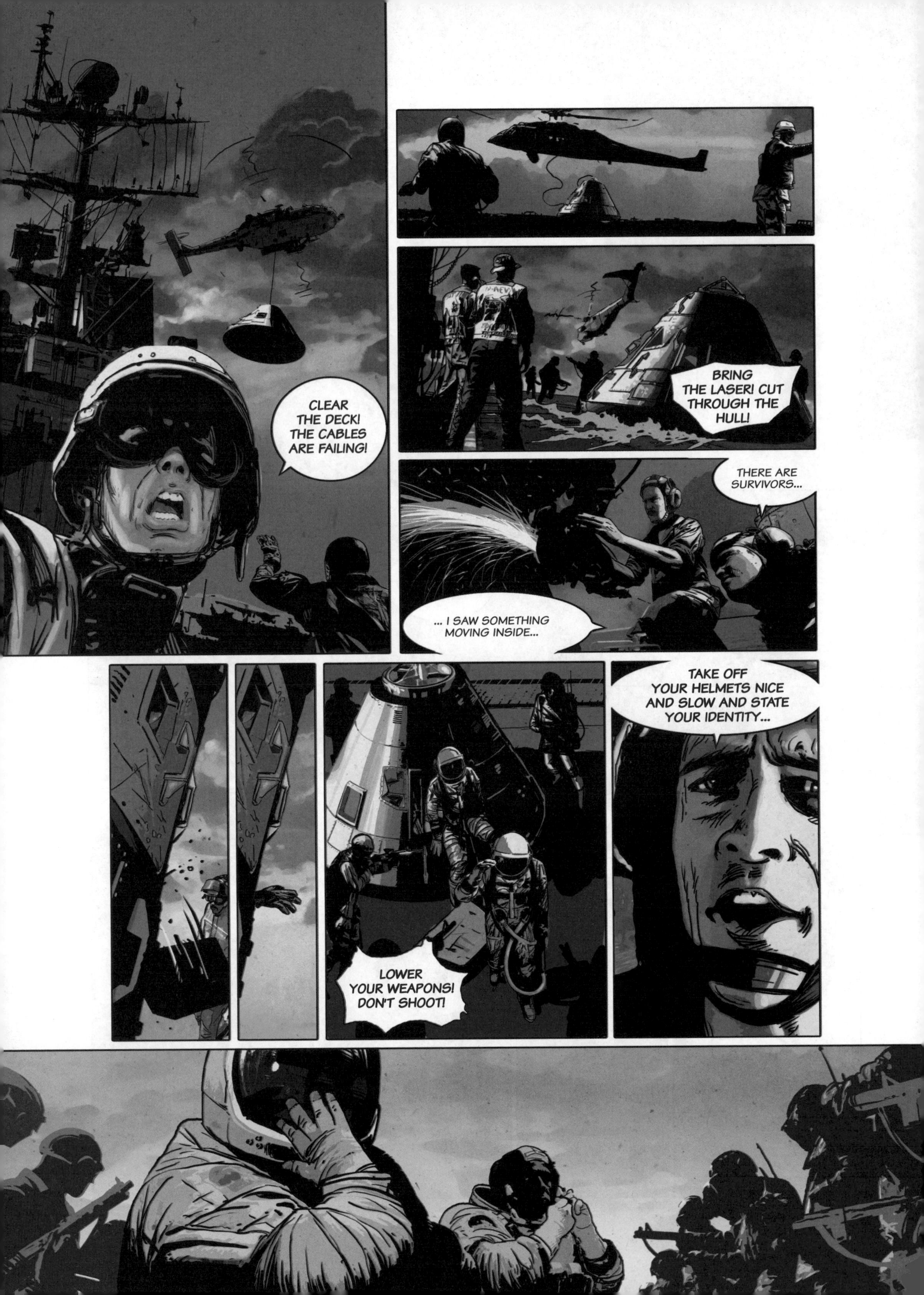
CLEAR THE DECK! THE CABLES ARE FAILING!
BRING THE LASER! CUT THROUGH THE HULL!
THERE ARE SURVIVORS...
... I SAW SOMETHING MOVING INSIDE...
LOWER YOUR WEAPONS! DON'T SHOOT!
TAKE OFF YOUR HELMETS NICE AND SLOW AND STATE YOUR IDENTITY...

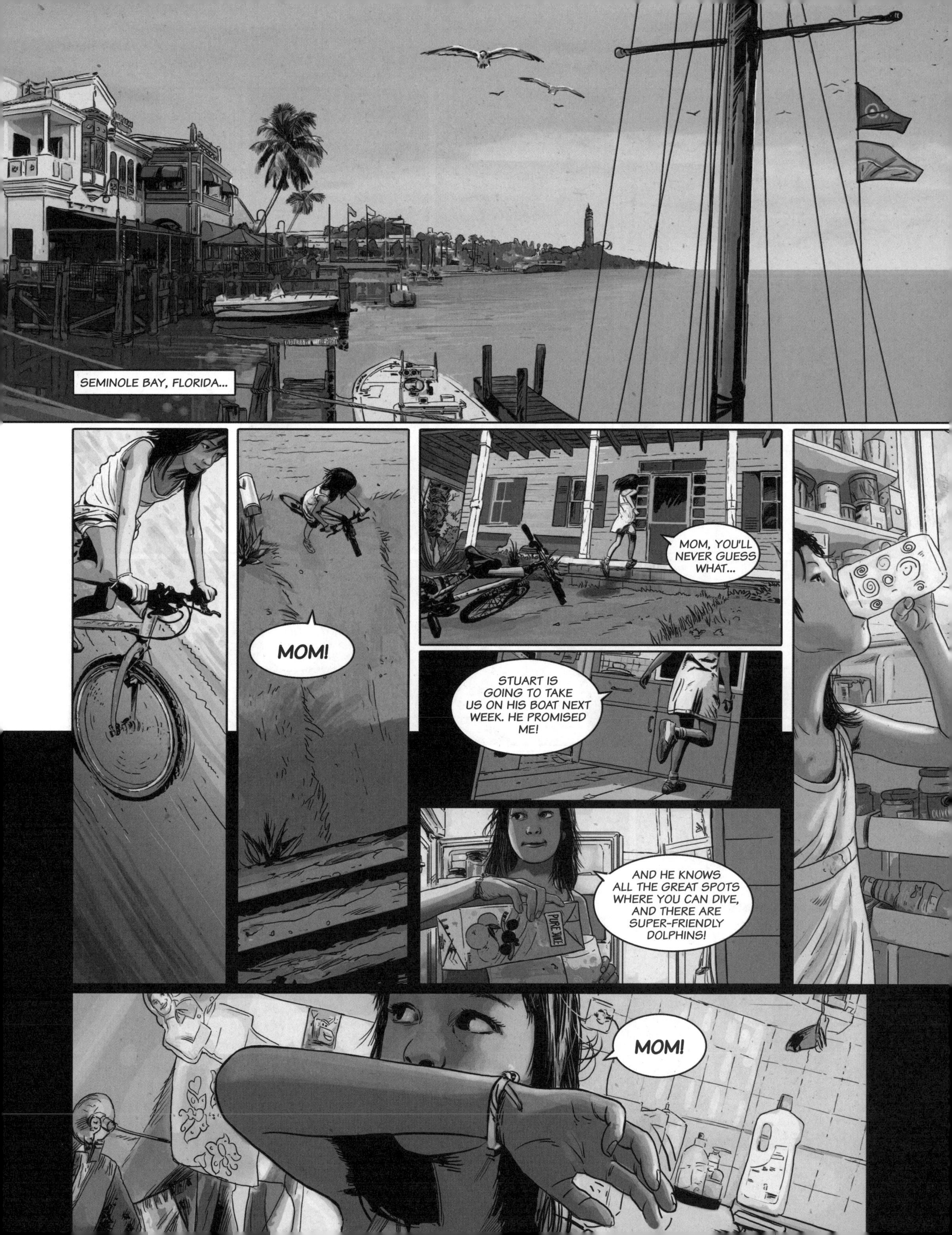
SEMINOLE BAY, FLORIDA...
MOM!
MOM, YOU'LL NEVER GUESS WHAT...
STUART IS GOING TO TAKE US ON HIS BOAT NEXT WEEK. HE PROMISED ME!
PURE JUICE
AND HE KNOWS ALL THE GREAT SPOTS WHERE YOU CAN DIVE, AND THERE ARE SUPER-FRIENDLY DOLPHINS!
MOM!

Helen Freeman
2351 sv postlewait
Florida
YOU GOT ANOTHER LETTER FOR YOUR WORK, DIDN'T YOU?
ARE YOU GOING TO GO ON ANOTHER MISSION?
NO, SOFIA...
THEN WHAT'S THIS LETTER FOR?
I'M NOT STUPID! IT'S GOT THE NASA LOGO ON IT!
IT'S A LETTER FROM WORK, YES, BUT I'M NOT GOING ON A MISSION...
THEN WHY ARE YOU CRYING? YOU SHOULD BE HAPPY, SINCE YOU PROMISED ME YOU WOULDN'T GO AWAY FOR A LONG TIME ANYMORE!
KNOWING YOUR STRONG MOTIVATION AND BRILLIANT SERVICE RECORD, I AM SURE YOU WILL BE UPSET TO LEARN THAT THE BUDGET CUTS OUR AGENCY HAS SUFFERED FOR THE PAST FIVE YEARS HAVE FORCED US TO PUSH ALL MARTIAN MISSIONS BACK BY 20 TO 30 YEARS.

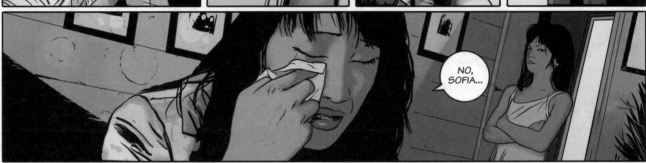

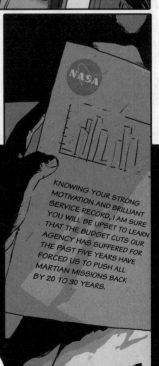

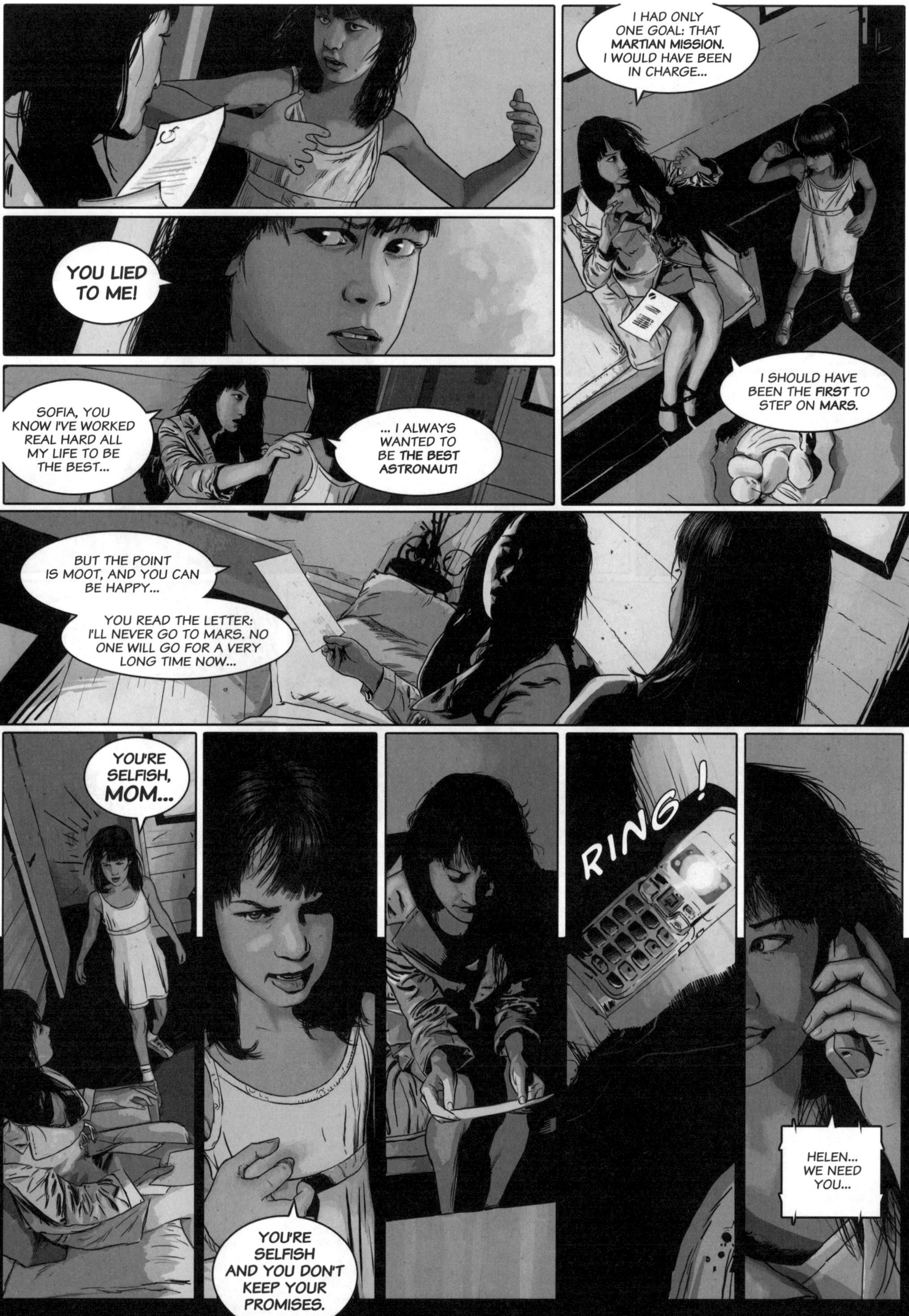
YOU LIED TO ME!
SOFIA, YOU KNOW I'VE WORKED REAL HARD ALL MY LIFE TO BE THE BEST...
... I ALWAYS WANTED TO BE THE BEST ASTRONAUT!
I HAD ONLY ONE GOAL: THAT MARTIAN MISSION. I WOULD HAVE BEEN IN CHARGE...
I SHOULD HAVE BEEN THE FIRST TO STEP ON MARS.
BUT THE POINT IS MOOT, AND YOU CAN BE HAPPY...
YOU READ THE LETTER: I'LL NEVER GO TO MARS. NO ONE WILL GO FOR A VERY LONG TIME NOW...
YOU'RE SELFISH, MOM...
YOU'RE SELFISH AND YOU DON'T KEEP YOUR PROMISES.
RING!
HELEN... WE NEED YOU...

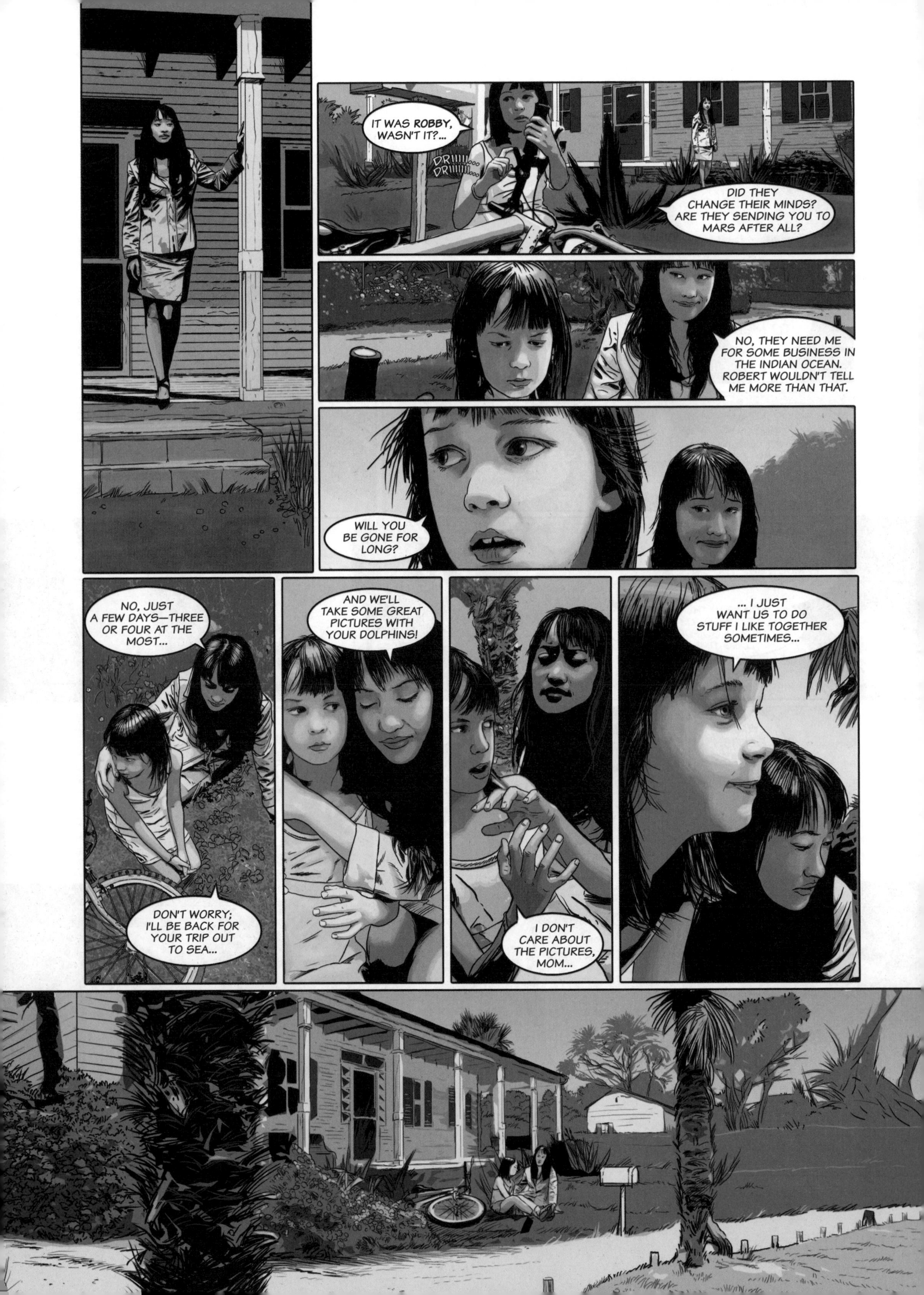
IT WAS ROBBY, WASN'T IT?...
DRIIIIII... DRIIIIII...
DID THEY CHANGE THEIR MINDS? ARE THEY SENDING YOU TO MARS AFTER ALL?
NO, THEY NEED ME FOR SOME BUSINESS IN THE INDIAN OCEAN. ROBERT WOULDN'T TELL ME MORE THAN THAT.
WILL YOU BE GONE FOR LONG?
NO, JUST A FEW DAYS—THREE OR FOUR AT THE MOST...
DON'T WORRY; I'LL BE BACK FOR YOUR TRIP OUT TO SEA...
AND WE'LL TAKE SOME GREAT PICTURES WITH YOUR DOLPHINS!
I DON'T CARE ABOUT THE PICTURES, MOM...
... I JUST WANT US TO DO STUFF I LIKE TOGETHER SOMETIMES...

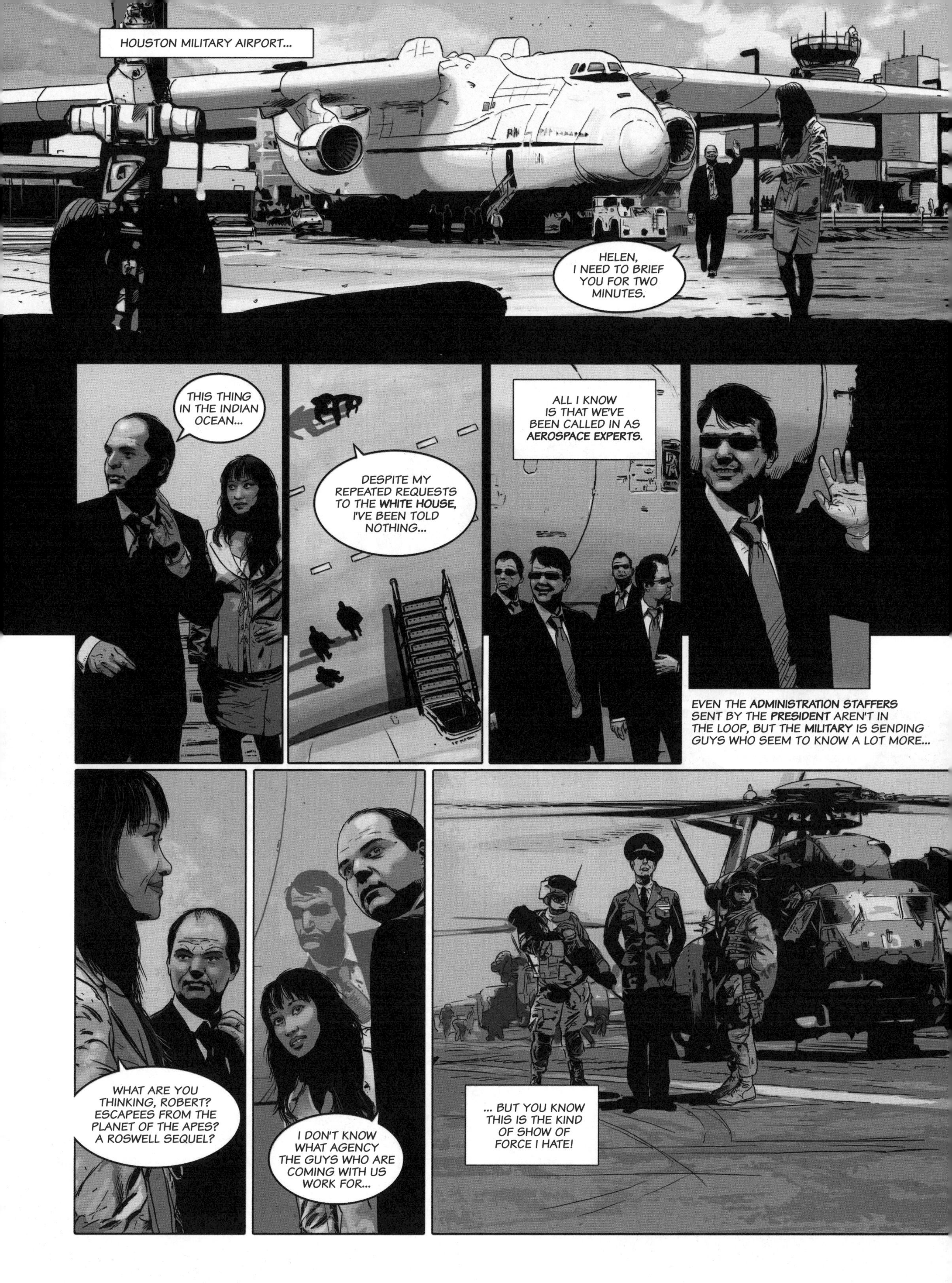

HOUSTON MILITARY AIRPORT...
HELEN, I NEED TO BRIEF YOU FOR TWO MINUTES.
THIS THING IN THE INDIAN OCEAN...
DESPITE MY REPEATED REQUESTS TO THE WHITE HOUSE, I'VE BEEN TOLD NOTHING...
ALL I KNOW IS THAT WE'VE BEEN CALLED IN AS AEROSPACE EXPERTS.
EVEN THE ADMINISTRATION STAFFERS SENT BY THE PRESIDENT AREN'T IN THE LOOP, BUT THE MILITARY IS SENDING GUYS WHO SEEM TO KNOW A LOT MORE...
WHAT ARE YOU THINKING, ROBERT? ESCAPEES FROM THE PLANET OF THE APES? A ROSWELL SEQUEL?
I DON'T KNOW WHAT AGENCY THE GUYS WHO ARE COMING WITH US WORK FOR...
... BUT YOU KNOW THIS IS THE KIND OF SHOW OF FORCE I HATE!

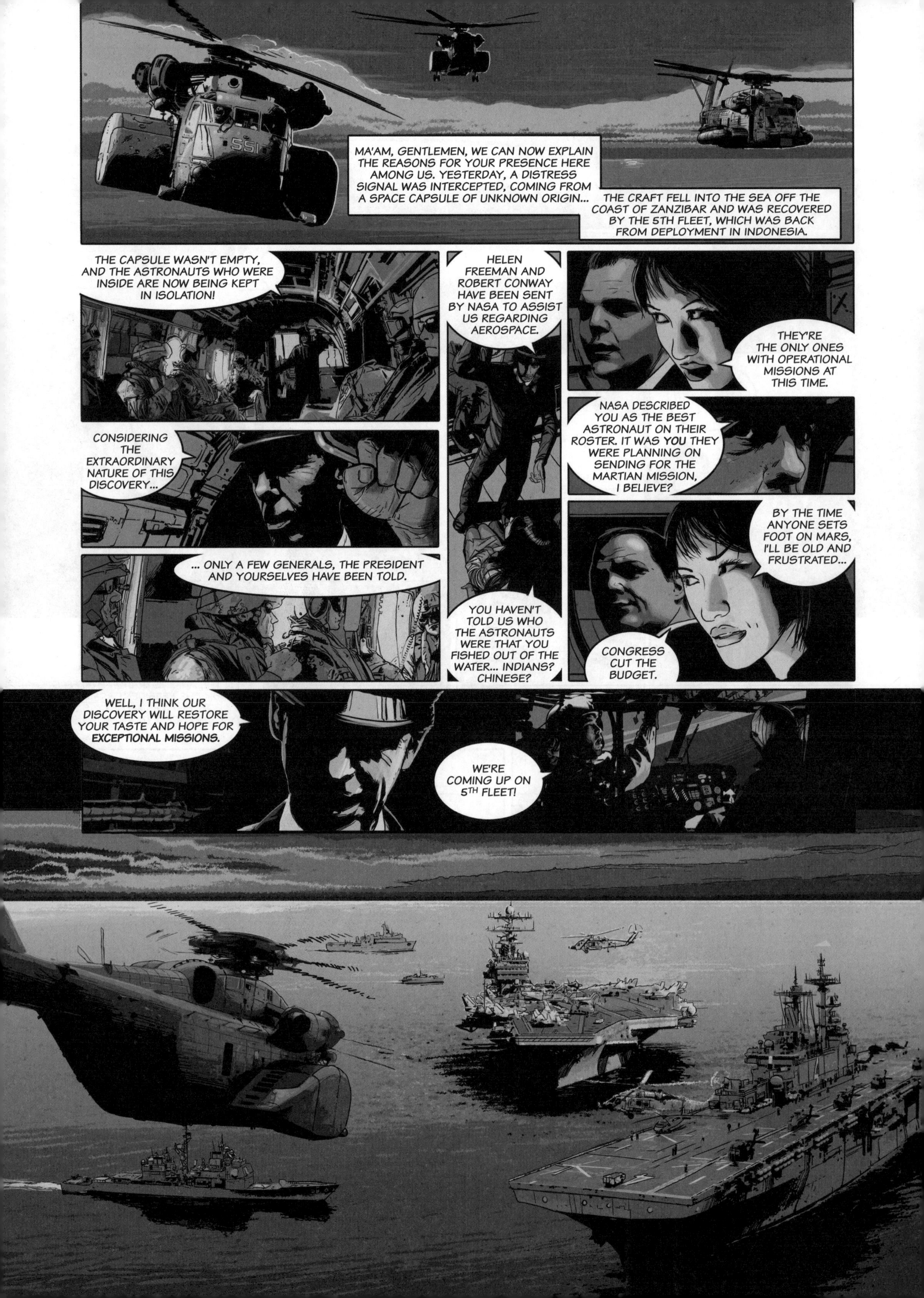
MA'AM, GENTLEMEN, WE CAN NOW EXPLAIN THE REASONS FOR YOUR PRESENCE HERE AMONG US. YESTERDAY, A DISTRESS SIGNAL WAS INTERCEPTED, COMING FROM A SPACE CAPSULE OF UNKNOWN ORIGIN...
THE CRAFT FELL INTO THE SEA OFF THE COAST OF ZANZIBAR AND WAS RECOVERED BY THE 5TH FLEET, WHICH WAS BACK FROM DEPLOYMENT IN INDONESIA.
THE CAPSULE WASN'T EMPTY, AND THE ASTRONAUTS WHO WERE INSIDE ARE NOW BEING KEPT IN ISOLATION!
CONSIDERING THE EXTRAORDINARY NATURE OF THIS DISCOVERY...
... ONLY A FEW GENERALS, THE PRESIDENT AND YOURSELVES HAVE BEEN TOLD.
HELEN FREEMAN AND ROBERT CONWAY HAVE BEEN SENT BY NASA TO ASSIST US REGARDING AEROSPACE.
YOU HAVEN'T TOLD US WHO THE ASTRONAUTS WERE THAT YOU FISHED OUT OF THE WATER... INDIANS? CHINESE?
THEY'RE THE ONLY ONES WITH OPERATIONAL MISSIONS AT THIS TIME.
NASA DESCRIBED YOU AS THE BEST ASTRONAUT ON THEIR ROSTER. IT WAS YOU THEY WERE PLANNING ON SENDING FOR THE MARTIAN MISSION, I BELIEVE?
BY THE TIME ANYONE SETS FOOT ON MARS, I'LL BE OLD AND FRUSTRATED...
CONGRESS CUT THE BUDGET.
WELL, I THINK OUR DISCOVERY WILL RESTORE YOUR TASTE AND HOPE FOR EXCEPTIONAL MISSIONS.
WE'RE COMING UP ON 5TH FLEET!

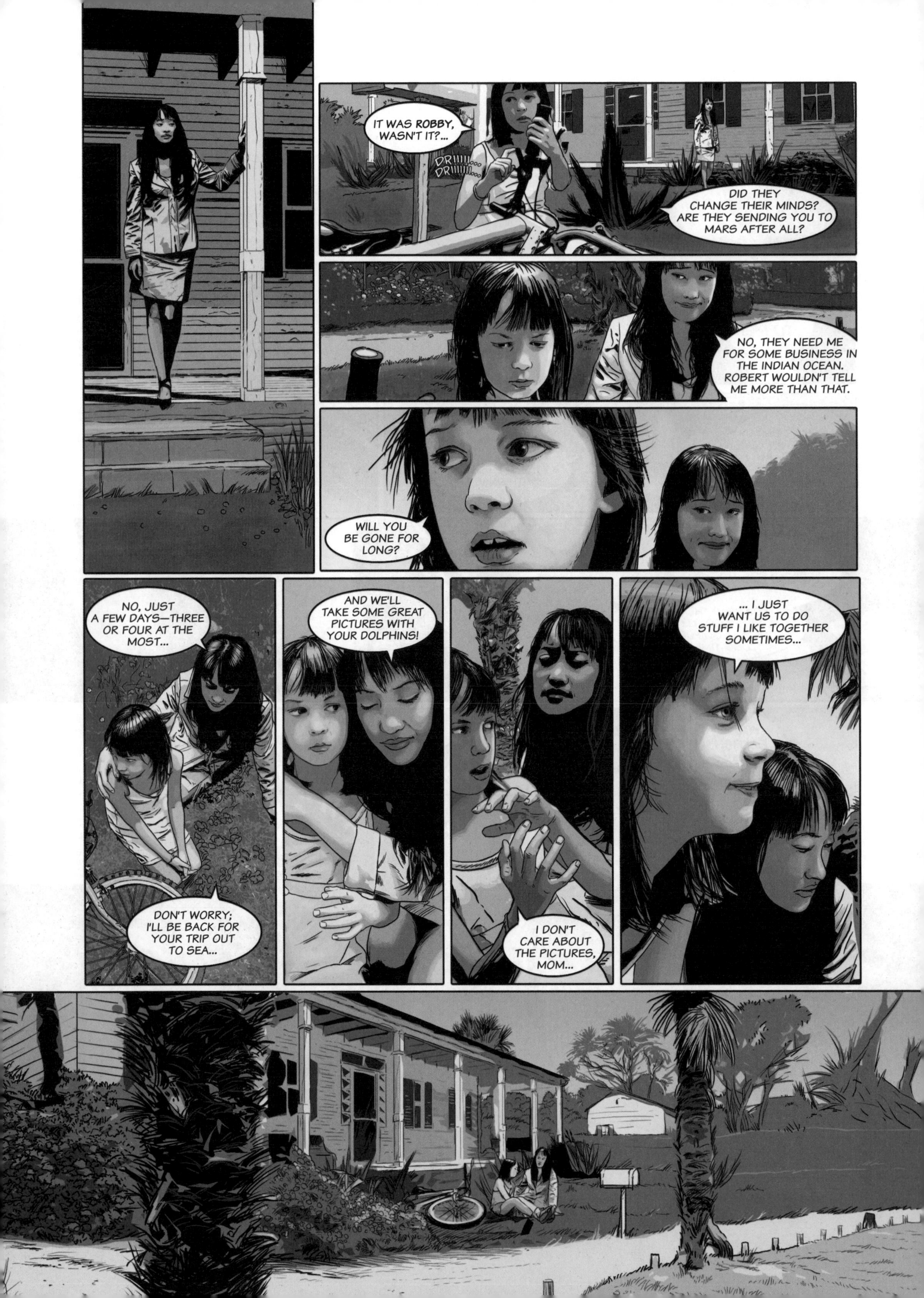
IT WAS ROBBY, WASN'T IT?...
DRIIIIII... DRIIIIII...
DID THEY CHANGE THEIR MINDS? ARE THEY SENDING YOU TO MARS AFTER ALL?
NO, THEY NEED ME FOR SOME BUSINESS IN THE INDIAN OCEAN. ROBERT WOULDN'T TELL ME MORE THAN THAT.
WILL YOU BE GONE FOR LONG?
NO, JUST A FEW DAYS—THREE OR FOUR AT THE MOST...
DON'T WORRY; I'LL BE BACK FOR YOUR TRIP OUT TO SEA...
AND WE'LL TAKE SOME GREAT PICTURES WITH YOUR DOLPHINS!
I DON'T CARE ABOUT THE PICTURES, MOM...
... I JUST WANT US TO DO STUFF I LIKE TOGETHER SOMETIMES...

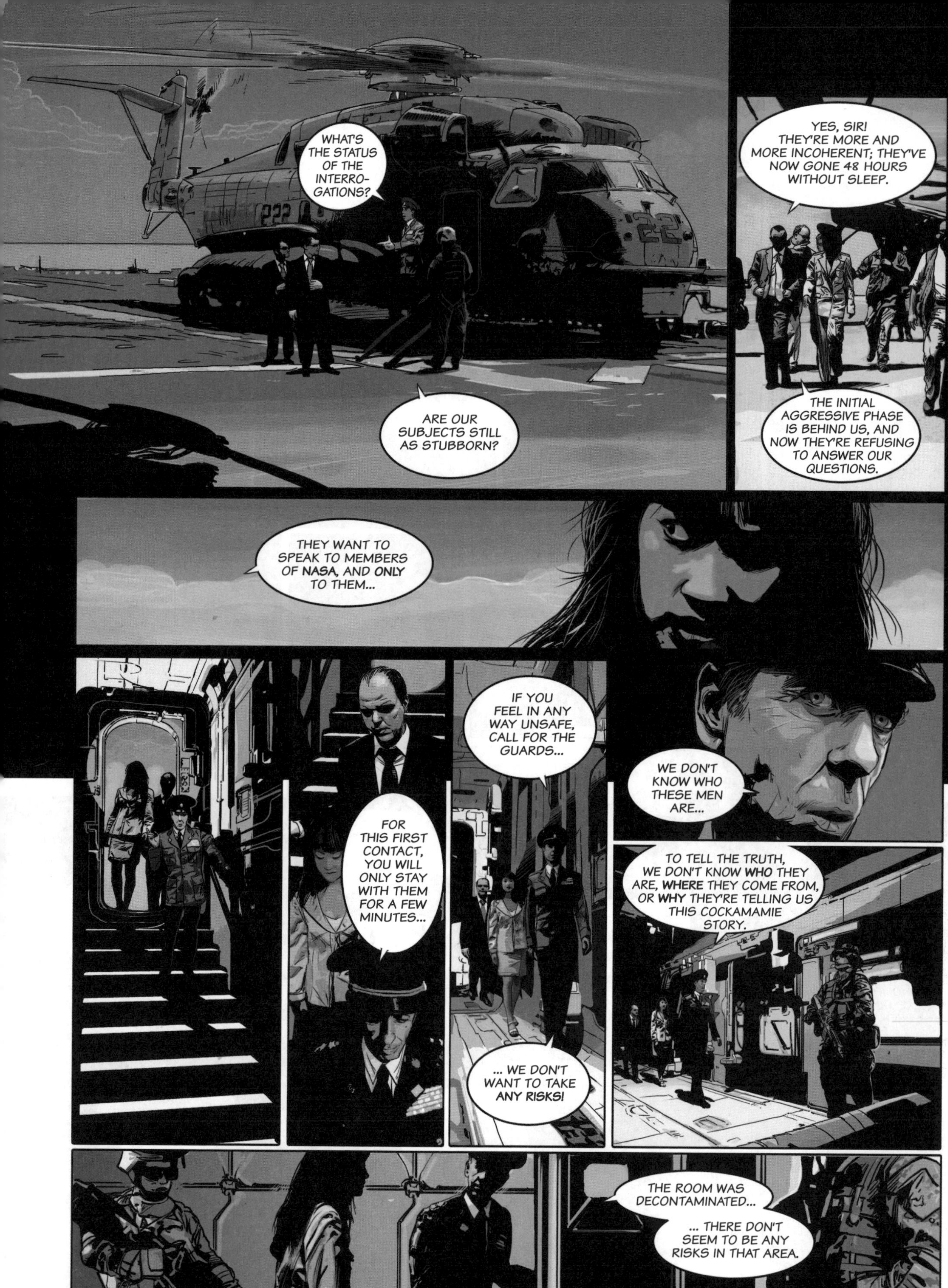
WHAT'S THE STATUS OF THE INTERRO-GATIONS?
ARE OUR SUBJECTS STILL AS STUBBORN?
YES, SIR! THEY'RE MORE AND MORE INCOHERENT; THEY'VE NOW GONE 48 HOURS WITHOUT SLEEP.
THE INITIAL AGGRESSIVE PHASE IS BEHIND US, AND NOW THEY'RE REFUSING TO ANSWER OUR QUESTIONS.
THEY WANT TO SPEAK TO MEMBERS OF NASA, AND ONLY TO THEM...
FOR THIS FIRST CONTACT, YOU WILL ONLY STAY WITH THEM FOR A FEW MINUTES...
IF YOU FEEL IN ANY WAY UNSAFE, CALL FOR THE GUARDS...
... WE DON'T WANT TO TAKE ANY RISKS!
WE DON'T KNOW WHO THESE MEN ARE...
TO TELL THE TRUTH, WE DON'T KNOW WHO THEY ARE, WHERE THEY COME FROM, OR WHY THEY'RE TELLING US THIS COCKAMAMIE STORY.
THE ROOM WAS DECONTAMINATED...
... THERE DON'T SEEM TO BE ANY RISKS IN THAT AREA.

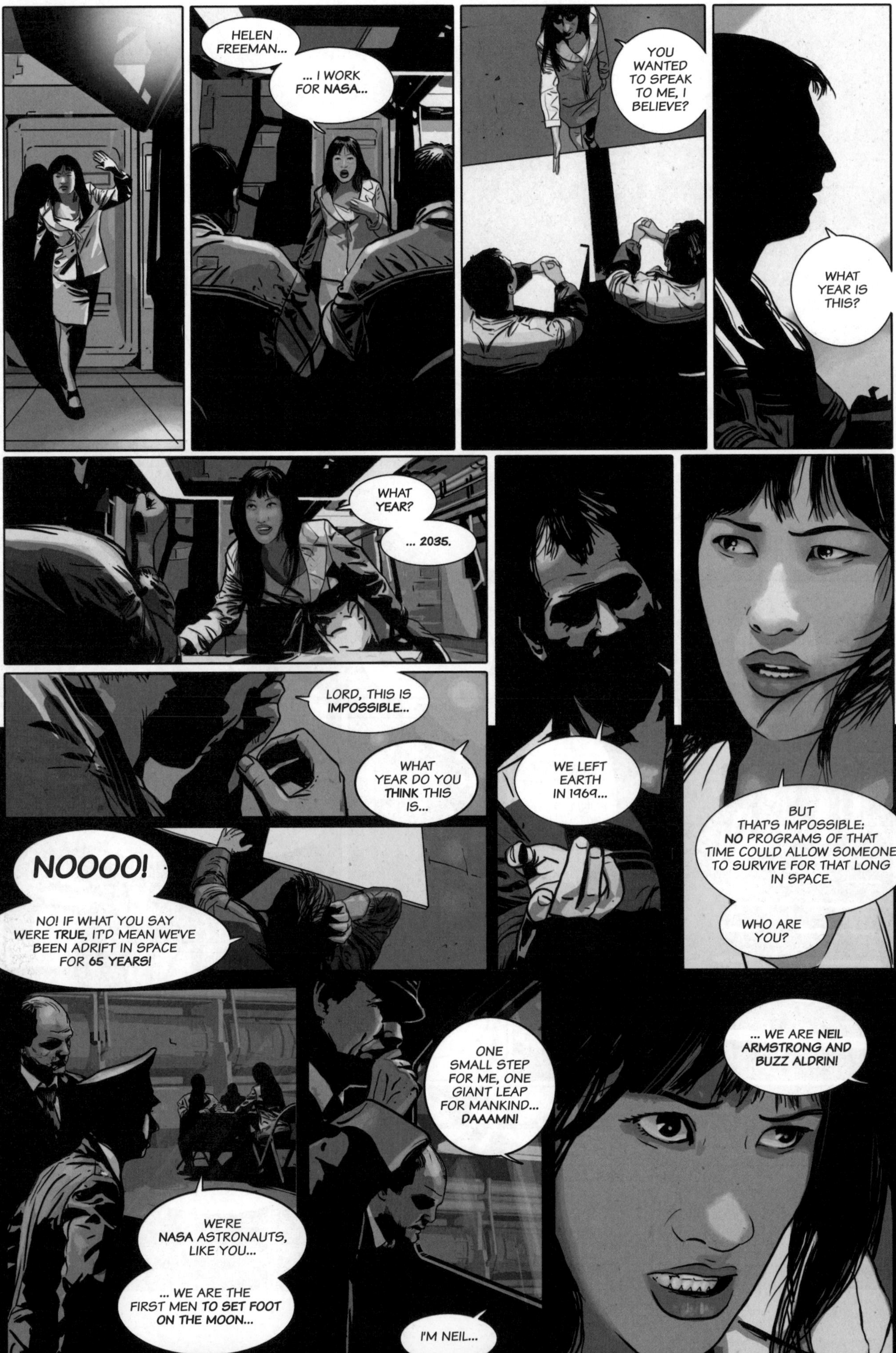
HELEN FREEMAN...
... I WORK FOR NASA...
YOU WANTED TO SPEAK TO ME, I BELIEVE?
WHAT YEAR IS THIS?
WHAT YEAR?
... 2035.
LORD, THIS IS IMPOSSIBLE...
WHAT YEAR DO YOU THINK THIS IS...
NOOOO!
NO! IF WHAT YOU SAY WERE TRUE, IT'D MEAN WE'VE BEEN ADRIFT IN SPACE FOR 65 YEARS!
WE LEFT EARTH IN 1969...
BUT THAT'S IMPOSSIBLE: NO PROGRAMS OF THAT TIME COULD ALLOW SOMEONE TO SURVIVE FOR THAT LONG IN SPACE.
WHO ARE YOU?
WE'RE NASA ASTRONAUTS, LIKE YOU...
... WE ARE THE FIRST MEN TO SET FOOT ON THE MOON...
ONE SMALL STEP FOR ME, ONE GIANT LEAP FOR MANKIND... DAAAMN!
I'M NEIL...
... WE ARE NEIL ARMSTRONG AND BUZZ ALDRIN!

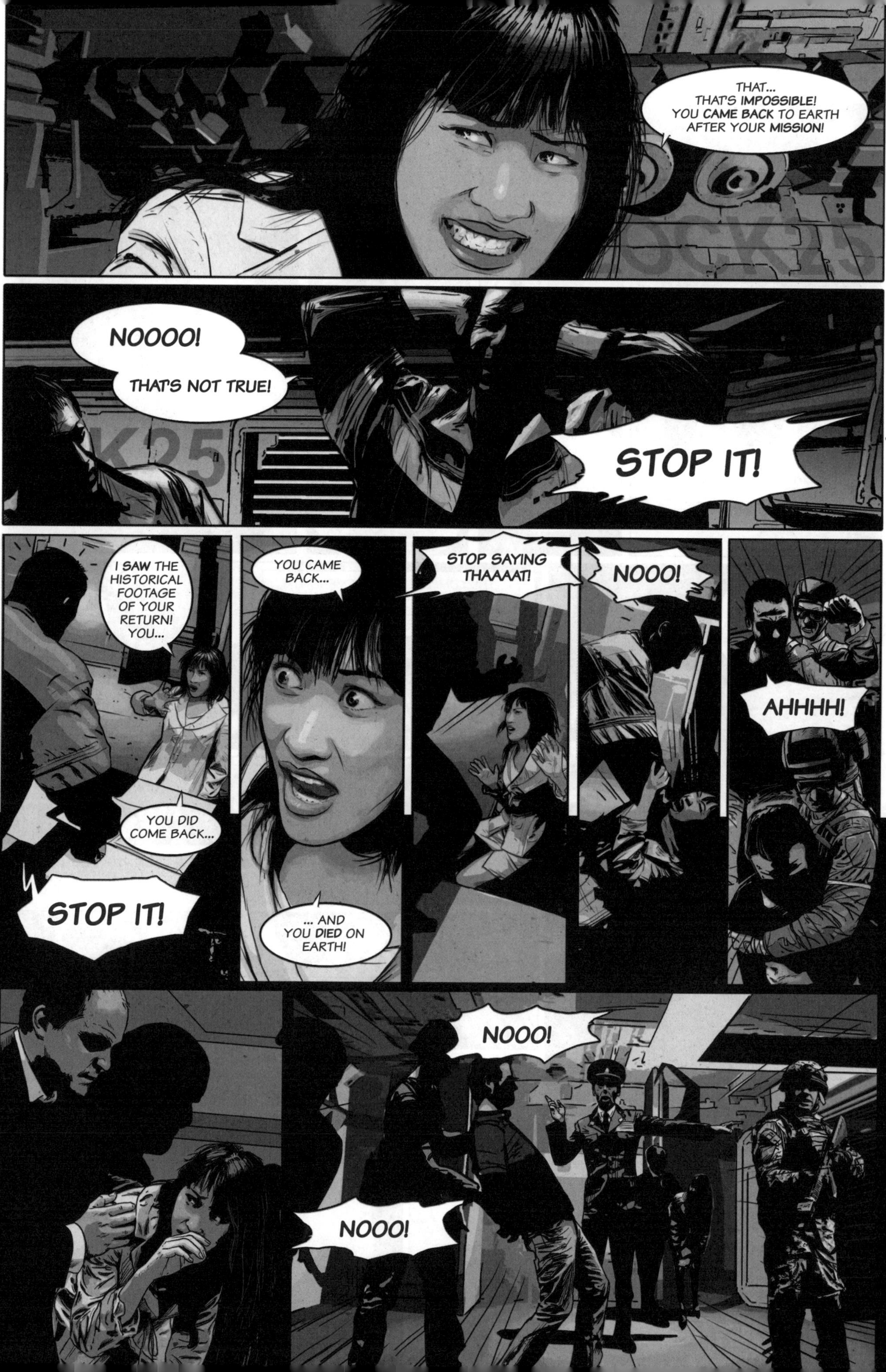
THAT... THAT'S IMPOSSIBLE! YOU CAME BACK TO EARTH AFTER YOUR MISSION!
NOOOO!
THAT'S NOT TRUE!
STOP IT!
I SAW THE HISTORICAL FOOTAGE OF YOUR RETURN! YOU...
YOU DID COME BACK...
STOP IT!
YOU CAME BACK...
... AND YOU DIED ON EARTH!
STOP SAYING THAAAAT!
NOOO!
AHHHH!
NOOO!
NOOO!

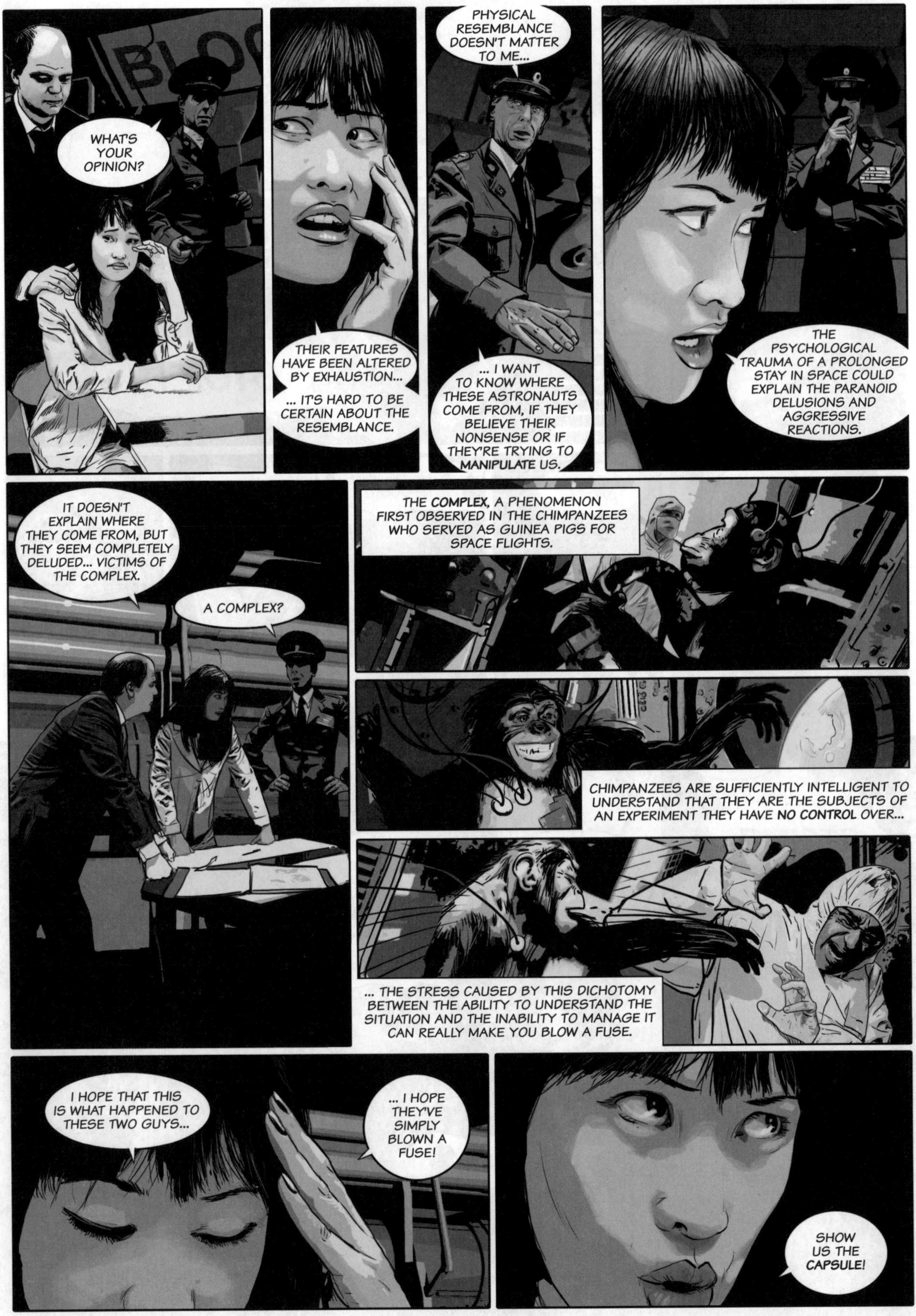
WHAT'S YOUR OPINION?
THEIR FEATURES HAVE BEEN ALTERED BY EXHAUSTION...
... IT'S HARD TO BE CERTAIN ABOUT THE RESEMBLANCE.
PHYSICAL RESEMBLANCE DOESN'T MATTER TO ME...
... I WANT TO KNOW WHERE THESE ASTRONAUTS COME FROM, IF THEY BELIEVE THEIR NONSENSE OR IF THEY'RE TRYING TO MANIPULATE US.
THE PSYCHOLOGICAL TRAUMA OF A PROLONGED STAY IN SPACE COULD EXPLAIN THE PARANOID DELUSIONS AND AGGRESSIVE REACTIONS.
IT DOESN'T EXPLAIN WHERE THEY COME FROM, BUT THEY SEEM COMPLETELY DELUDED... VICTIMS OF THE COMPLEX.
A COMPLEX?
THE COMPLEX, A PHENOMENON FIRST OBSERVED IN THE CHIMPANZEES WHO SERVED AS GUINEA PIGS FOR SPACE FLIGHTS.
CHIMPANZEES ARE SUFFICIENTLY INTELLIGENT TO UNDERSTAND THAT THEY ARE THE SUBJECTS OF AN EXPERIMENT THEY HAVE NO CONTROL OVER...
... THE STRESS CAUSED BY THIS DICHOTOMY BETWEEN THE ABILITY TO UNDERSTAND THE SITUATION AND THE INABILITY TO MANAGE IT CAN REALLY MAKE YOU BLOW A FUSE.
I HOPE THAT THIS IS WHAT HAPPENED TO THESE TWO GUYS...
... I HOPE THEY'VE SIMPLY BLOWN A FUSE!
SHOW US THE CAPSULE!

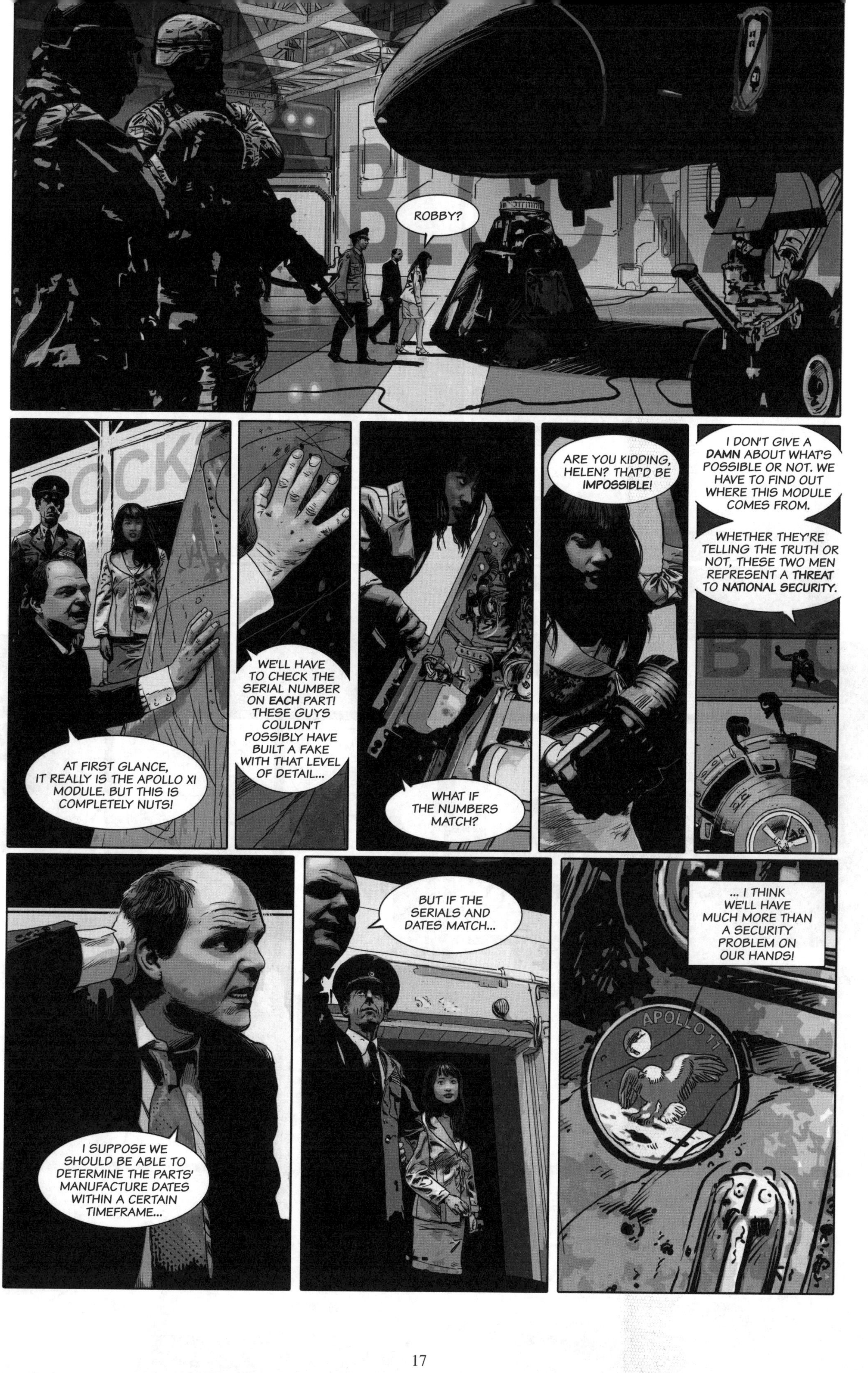
ROBBY?
AT FIRST GLANCE, IT REALLY IS THE APOLLO XI MODULE. BUT THIS IS COMPLETELY NUTS!
WE'LL HAVE TO CHECK THE SERIAL NUMBER ON EACH PART! THESE GUYS COULDN'T POSSIBLY HAVE BUILT A FAKE WITH THAT LEVEL OF DETAIL...
WHAT IF THE NUMBERS MATCH?
ARE YOU KIDDING, HELEN? THAT'D BE IMPOSSIBLE!
I DON'T GIVE A DAMN ABOUT WHAT'S POSSIBLE OR NOT. WE HAVE TO FIND OUT WHERE THIS MODULE COMES FROM.
WHETHER THEY'RE TELLING THE TRUTH OR NOT, THESE TWO MEN REPRESENT A THREAT TO NATIONAL SECURITY.
I SUPPOSE WE SHOULD BE ABLE TO DETERMINE THE PARTS' MANUFACTURE DATES WITHIN A CERTAIN TIMEFRAME...
BUT IF THE SERIALS AND DATES MATCH...
... I THINK WE'LL HAVE MUCH MORE THAN A SECURITY PROBLEM ON OUR HANDS!
APOLLO 11

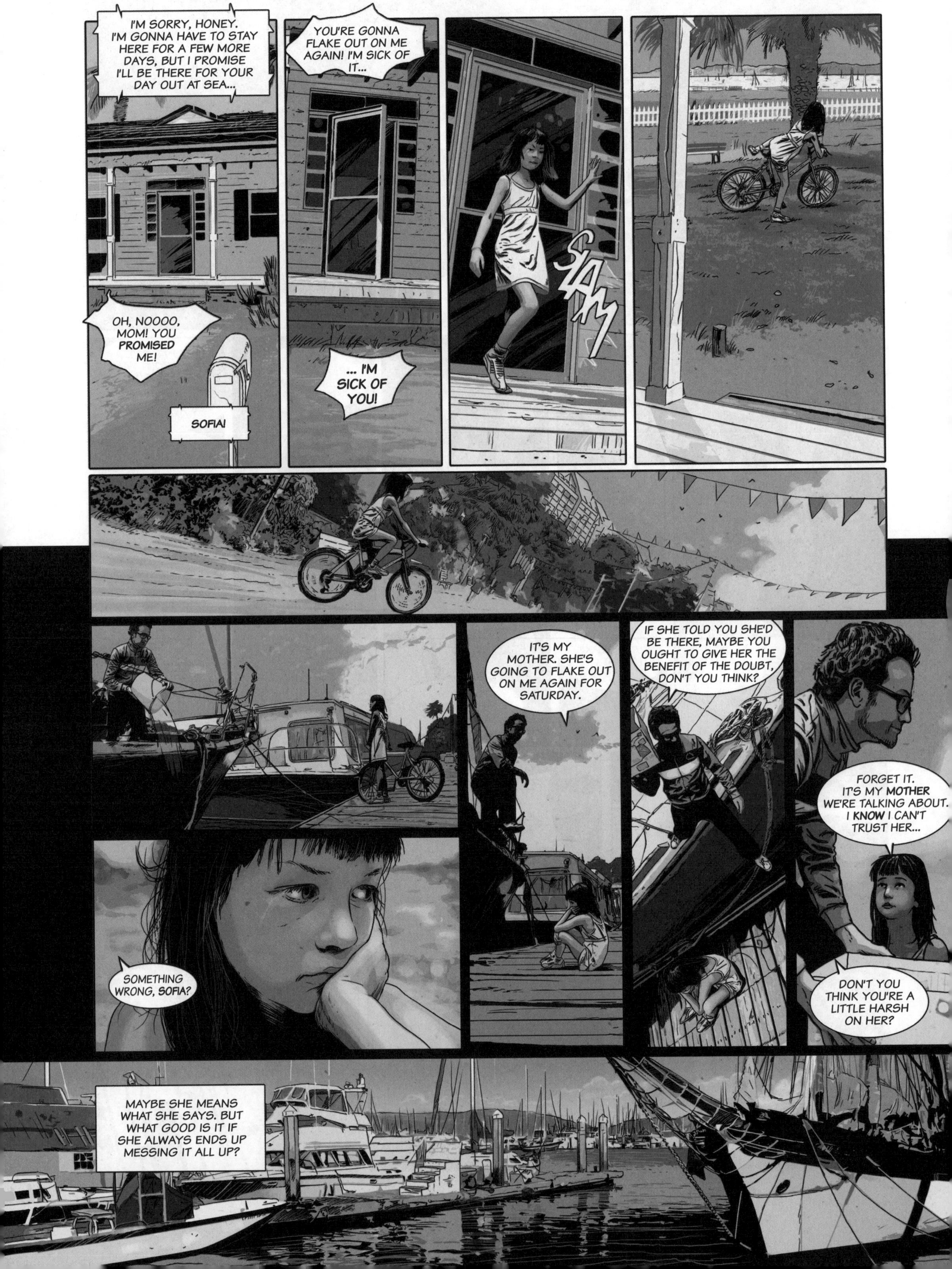
I'M SORRY, HONEY. I'M GONNA HAVE TO STAY HERE FOR A FEW MORE DAYS, BUT I PROMISE I'LL BE THERE FOR YOUR DAY OUT AT SEA...
OH, NOOOO, MOM! YOU PROMISED ME!
SOFIA!
YOU'RE GONNA FLAKE OUT ON ME AGAIN! I'M SICK OF IT...
... I'M SICK OF YOU!
SLAM
SOMETHING WRONG, SOFIA?
IT'S MY MOTHER. SHE'S GOING TO FLAKE OUT ON ME AGAIN FOR SATURDAY.
IF SHE TOLD YOU SHE'D BE THERE, MAYBE YOU OUGHT TO GIVE HER THE BENEFIT OF THE DOUBT, DON'T YOU THINK?
FORGET IT. IT'S MY MOTHER WE'RE TALKING ABOUT. I KNOW I CAN'T TRUST HER...
DON'T YOU THINK YOU'RE A LITTLE HARSH ON HER?
MAYBE SHE MEANS WHAT SHE SAYS. BUT WHAT GOOD IS IT IF SHE ALWAYS ENDS UP MESSING IT ALL UP?

RED HILLS CREEK MILITARY BASE, COLORADO

HERE WE ARE, HELEN...

... FROM NOW ON, IT'S THE "CREWCUTS" FROM SPECIAL OPS WHO ARE IN CHARGE.

THEY'LL TAKE THE MODULE APART...

... AND TAKE DOWN THE SERIAL NUMBER OF EACH PART.

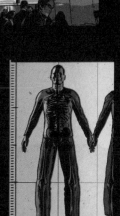

THEY MIGHT EVEN BE ABLE TO COMPARE THE **BIOMETRIC DATA** ORIGINALLY COLLECTED FROM ALDRIN AND ARMSTRONG WITH

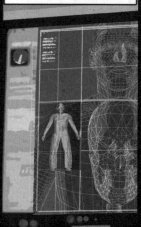

SUCH A COMPARISON SHOULD BE ENOUGH TO DEMONSTRATE THE FRAUD...

IT WON'T SATISFY KONRAD STEALBERG, BUT AT LEAST IT WILL TAKE NASA OUT OF THE SPOTLIGHT.

..Matching.. ....Data ......To find ....Neil .Armstrong

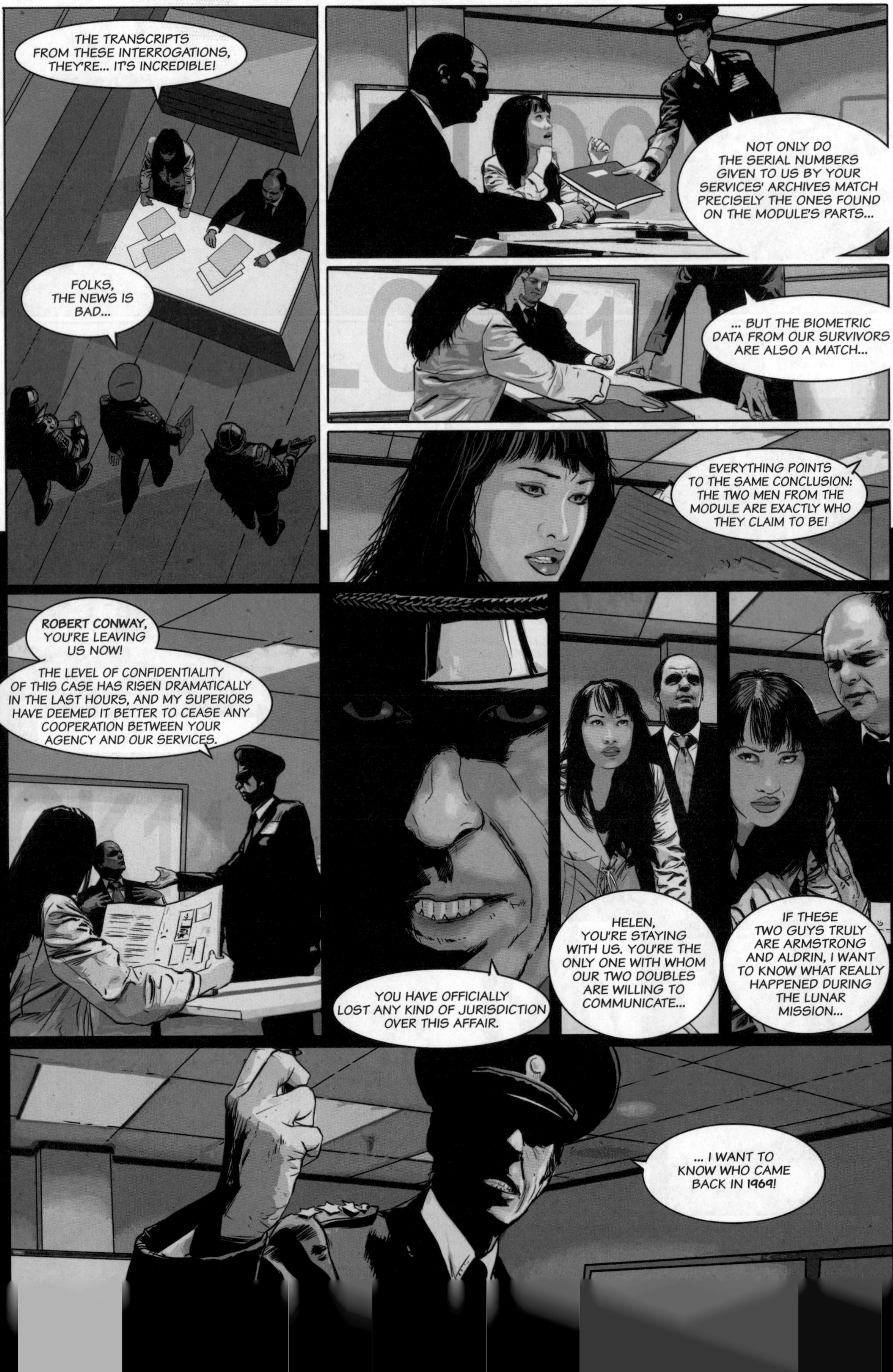
THE TRANSCRIPTS FROM THESE INTERROGATIONS, THEY'RE... IT'S INCREDIBLE!
FOLKS, THE NEWS IS BAD...
NOT ONLY DO THE SERIAL NUMBERS GIVEN TO US BY YOUR SERVICES' ARCHIVES MATCH PRECISELY THE ONES FOUND ON THE MODULE'S PARTS...
... BUT THE BIOMETRIC DATA FROM OUR SURVIVORS ARE ALSO A MATCH...
EVERYTHING POINTS TO THE SAME CONCLUSION: THE TWO MEN FROM THE MODULE ARE EXACTLY WHO THEY CLAIM TO BE!
ROBERT CONWAY, YOU'RE LEAVING US NOW!
THE LEVEL OF CONFIDENTIALITY OF THIS CASE HAS RISEN DRAMATICALLY IN THE LAST HOURS, AND MY SUPERIORS HAVE DEEMED IT BETTER TO CEASE ANY COOPERATION BETWEEN YOUR AGENCY AND OUR SERVICES.
YOU HAVE OFFICIALLY LOST ANY KIND OF JURISDICTION OVER THIS AFFAIR.
HELEN, YOU'RE STAYING WITH US. YOU'RE THE ONLY ONE WITH WHOM OUR TWO DOUBLES ARE WILLING TO COMMUNICATE...
IF THESE TWO GUYS TRULY ARE ARMSTRONG AND ALDRIN, I WANT TO KNOW WHAT REALLY HAPPENED DURING THE LUNAR MISSION...
... I WANT TO KNOW WHO CAME BACK IN 1969!

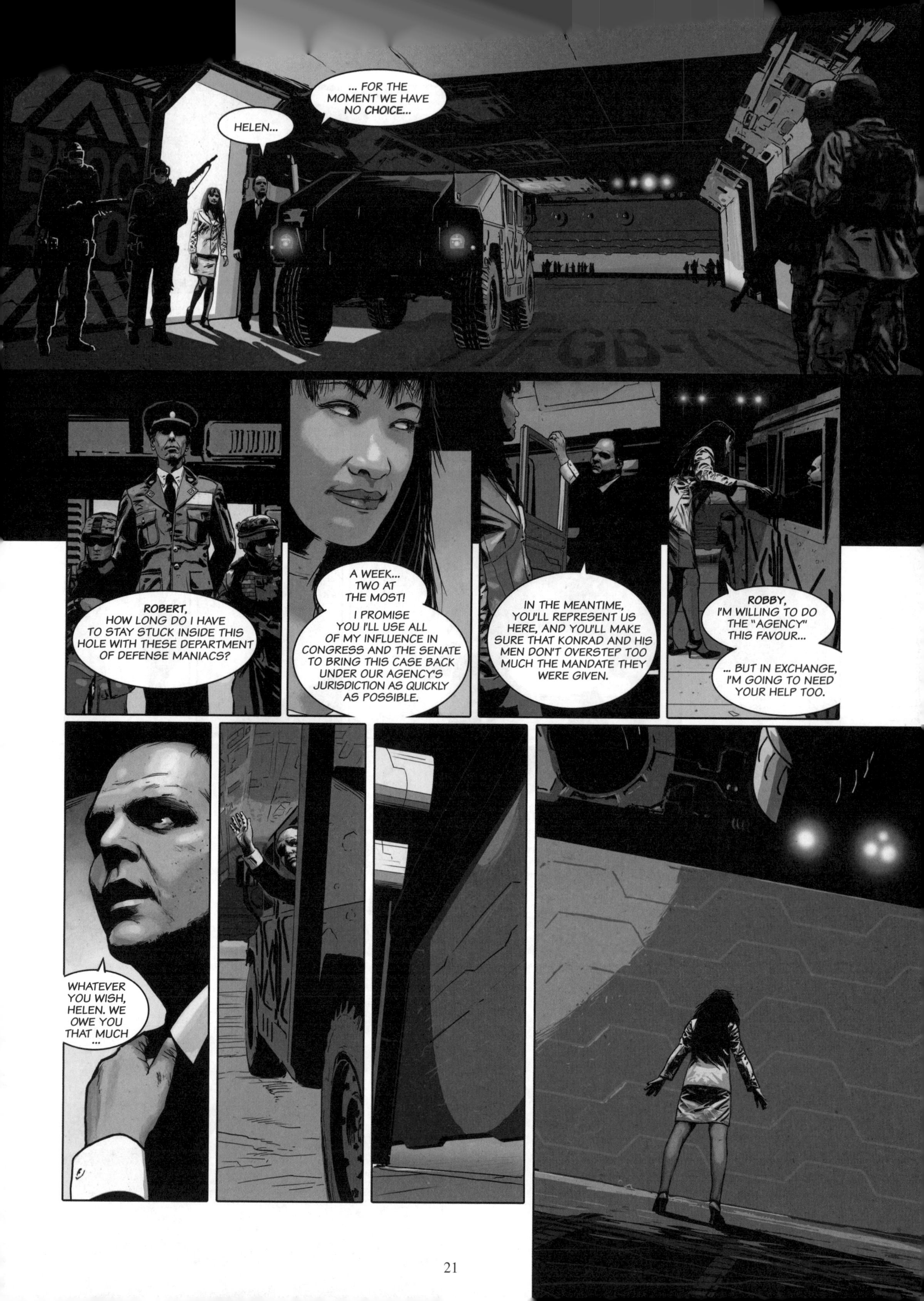
HELEN...
... FOR THE MOMENT WE HAVE NO CHOICE...
ROBERT, HOW LONG DO I HAVE TO STAY STUCK INSIDE THIS HOLE WITH THESE DEPARTMENT OF DEFENSE MANIACS?
A WEEK... TWO AT THE MOST!
I PROMISE YOU I'LL USE ALL OF MY INFLUENCE IN CONGRESS AND THE SENATE TO BRING THIS CASE BACK UNDER OUR AGENCY'S JURISDICTION AS QUICKLY AS POSSIBLE.
IN THE MEANTIME, YOU'LL REPRESENT US HERE, AND YOU'LL MAKE SURE THAT KONRAD AND HIS MEN DON'T OVERSTEP TOO MUCH THE MANDATE THEY WERE GIVEN.
ROBBY, I'M WILLING TO DO THE "AGENCY" THIS FAVOUR...
... BUT IN EXCHANGE, I'M GOING TO NEED YOUR HELP TOO.
WHATEVER YOU WISH, HELEN. WE OWE YOU THAT MUCH ...

ROBERT, RIGHT AFTER YOUR TRIP TO WASHINGTON, I WANT YOU TO EXPLAIN TO MY DAUGHTER WHY I'M STUCK HERE...

... I WANT HER TO UNDERSTAND THAT IT WASN'T MY FAULT, FOR ONCE!

... IT WILL COST YOU ONE DAY AT SEA WITH THE DOLPHINS, AND A PHOTO SHOOT WITH MY DAUGHTER.

WHATEVER YOU WISH, HELEN...

SOFIIIIA?! IT'S UNCLE ROB...

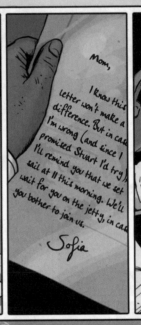
Mom,

I know this letter won't make a difference. But in case I'm wrong (and since I promised Stuart I'd try) I'll remind you that we set sail at 11 this morning. We'll wait for you on the jetty, in case you bother to join us.

Sofia

DAMMIT!

DAMMIT, DAMMIT, DAMMIT!

SOFIA?

IT'S ALMOST 11, SOFIA. I'M SORRY...

IF WE DON'T LEAVE NOW, WE RUN THE RISK OF MISSING THE DOLPHINS...

BUT WE CAN CANCEL IF YOU'D PREFER!

NO, STUART, LET'S GO...

... ANYWAY, I KNEW SHE WOULDN'T COME.

THERE'S ALWAYS A GOOD REASON...

... IT'S LIKE WITH MY DAD. SHE PROBABLY DROVE HIM CRAZY TOO...

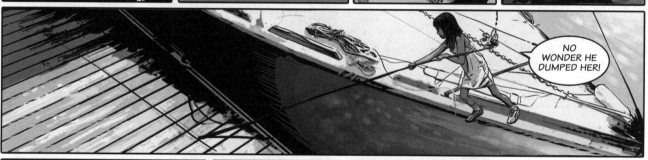

NO WONDER HE DUMPED HER!

... HNH...

... HNH... NN...

CRAP!

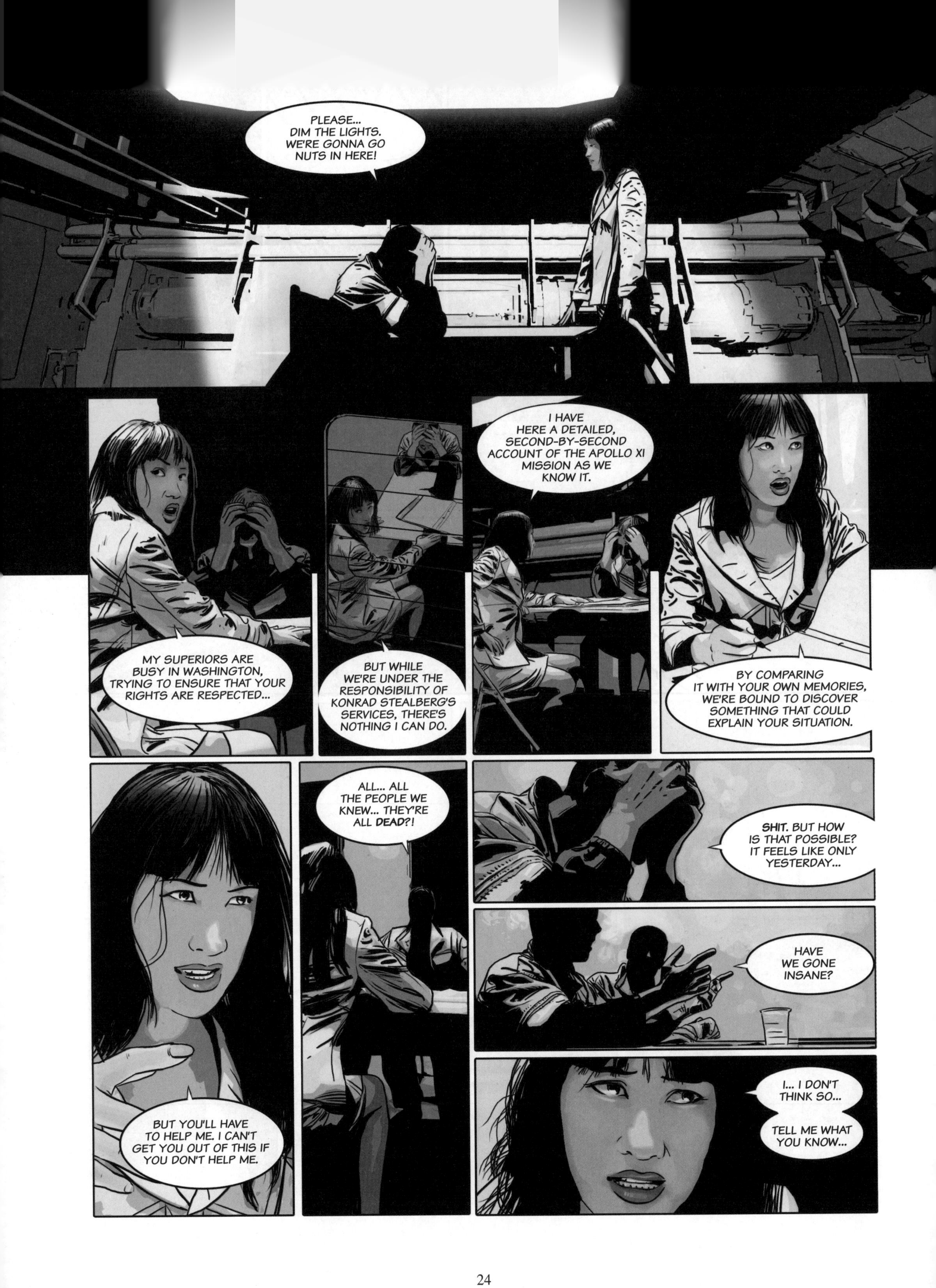
PLEASE... DIM THE LIGHTS. WE'RE GONNA GO NUTS IN HERE!
MY SUPERIORS ARE BUSY IN WASHINGTON, TRYING TO ENSURE THAT YOUR RIGHTS ARE RESPECTED...
BUT WHILE WE'RE UNDER THE RESPONSIBILITY OF KONRAD STEALBERG'S SERVICES, THERE'S NOTHING I CAN DO.
I HAVE HERE A DETAILED, SECOND-BY-SECOND ACCOUNT OF THE APOLLO XI MISSION AS WE KNOW IT.
BY COMPARING IT WITH YOUR OWN MEMORIES, WE'RE BOUND TO DISCOVER SOMETHING THAT COULD EXPLAIN YOUR SITUATION.
BUT YOU'LL HAVE TO HELP ME. I CAN'T GET YOU OUT OF THIS IF YOU DON'T HELP ME.
ALL... ALL THE PEOPLE WE KNEW... THEY'RE ALL **DEAD**?!
SHIT. BUT HOW IS THAT POSSIBLE? IT FEELS LIKE ONLY YESTERDAY...
HAVE WE GONE INSANE?
I... I DON'T THINK SO...
TELL ME WHAT YOU KNOW...

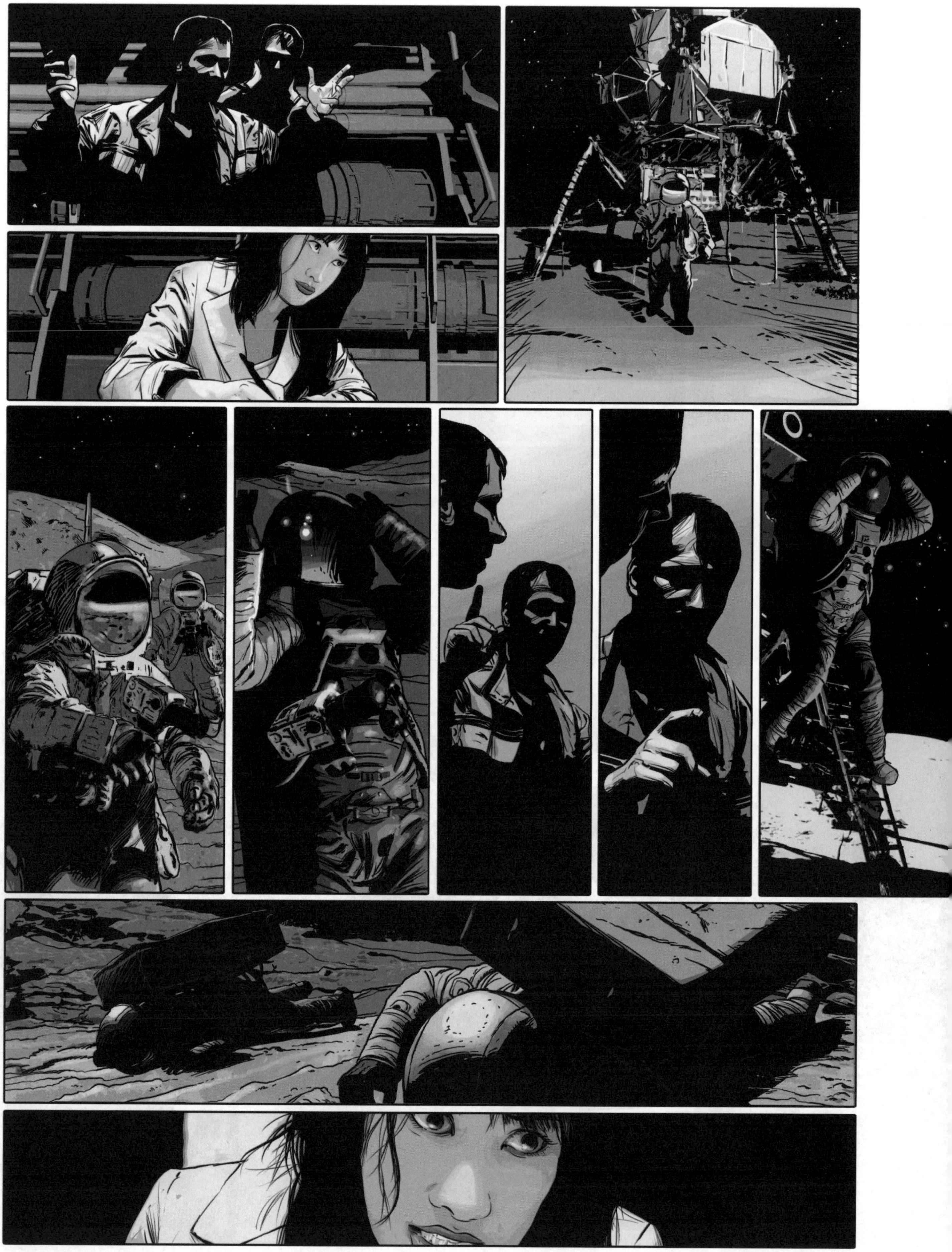

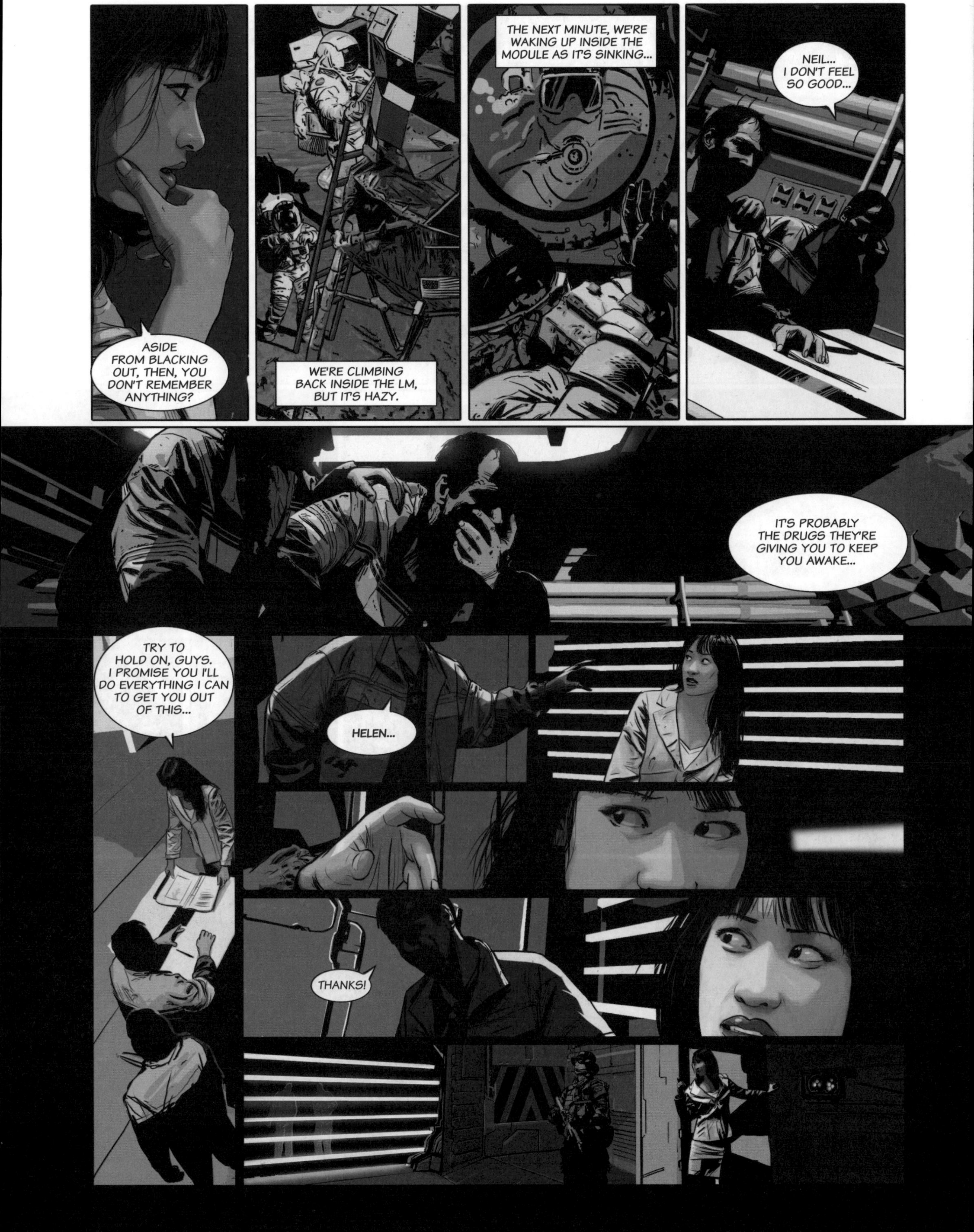

ASIDE FROM BLACKING OUT, THEN, YOU DON'T REMEMBER ANYTHING?
WE'RE CLIMBING BACK INSIDE THE LM, BUT IT'S HAZY.
THE NEXT MINUTE, WE'RE WAKING UP INSIDE THE MODULE AS IT'S SINKING...
NEIL... I DON'T FEEL SO GOOD...
IT'S PROBABLY THE DRUGS THEY'RE GIVING YOU TO KEEP YOU AWAKE...
TRY TO HOLD ON, GUYS. I PROMISE YOU I'LL DO EVERYTHING I CAN TO GET YOU OUT OF THIS...
HELEN...
THANKS!

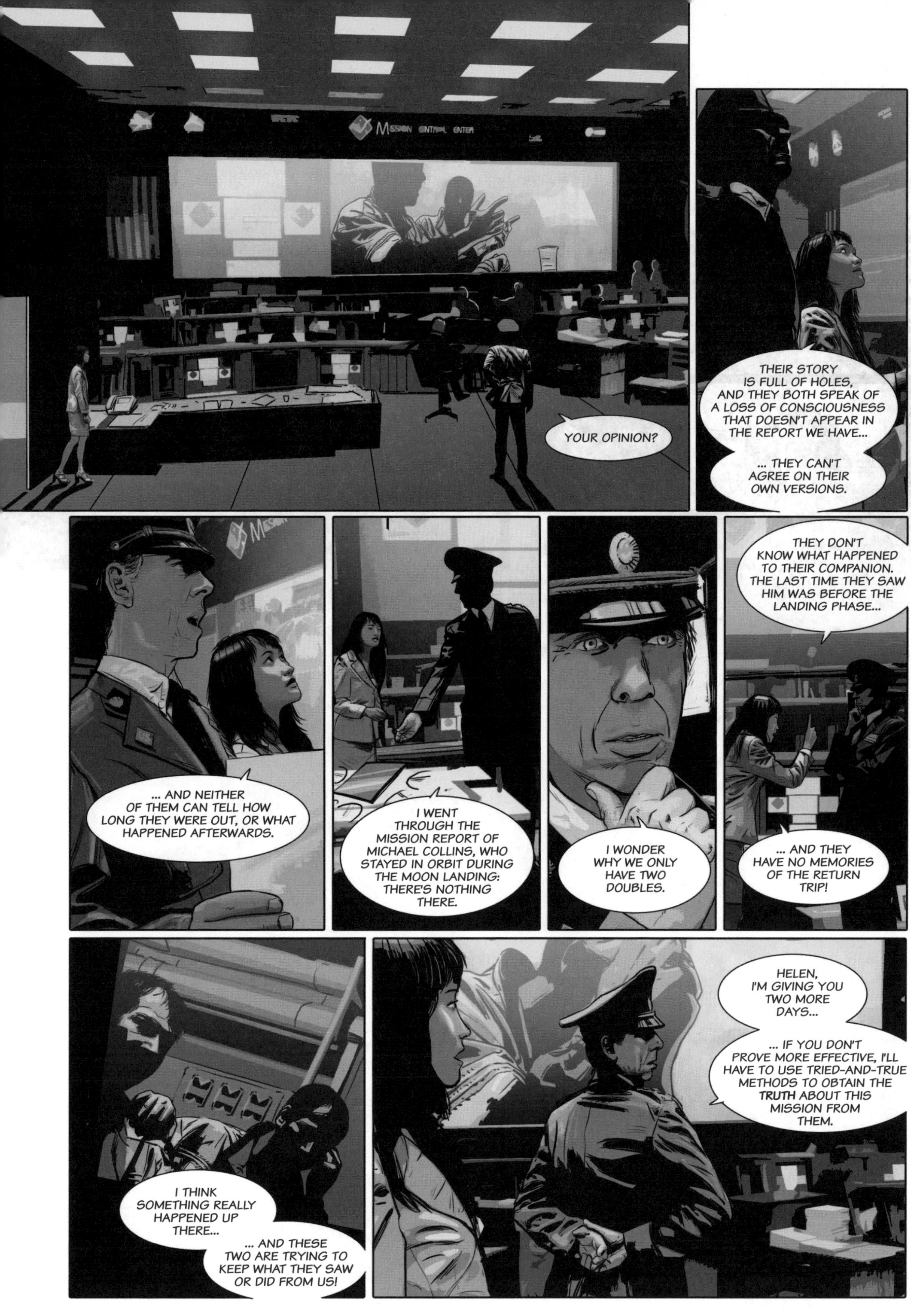

YOUR OPINION?
THEIR STORY IS FULL OF HOLES, AND THEY BOTH SPEAK OF A LOSS OF CONSCIOUSNESS THAT DOESN'T APPEAR IN THE REPORT WE HAVE...
... THEY CAN'T AGREE ON THEIR OWN VERSIONS.
... AND NEITHER OF THEM CAN TELL HOW LONG THEY WERE OUT, OR WHAT HAPPENED AFTERWARDS.
I WENT THROUGH THE MISSION REPORT OF MICHAEL COLLINS, WHO STAYED IN ORBIT DURING THE MOON LANDING: THERE'S NOTHING THERE.
I WONDER WHY WE ONLY HAVE TWO DOUBLES.
THEY DON'T KNOW WHAT HAPPENED TO THEIR COMPANION. THE LAST TIME THEY SAW HIM WAS BEFORE THE LANDING PHASE...
... AND THEY HAVE NO MEMORIES OF THE RETURN TRIP!
I THINK SOMETHING REALLY HAPPENED UP THERE...
... AND THESE TWO ARE TRYING TO KEEP WHAT THEY SAW OR DID FROM US!
HELEN, I'M GIVING YOU TWO MORE DAYS...
... IF YOU DON'T PROVE MORE EFFECTIVE, I'LL HAVE TO USE TRIED-AND-TRUE METHODS TO OBTAIN THE TRUTH ABOUT THIS MISSION FROM THEM.

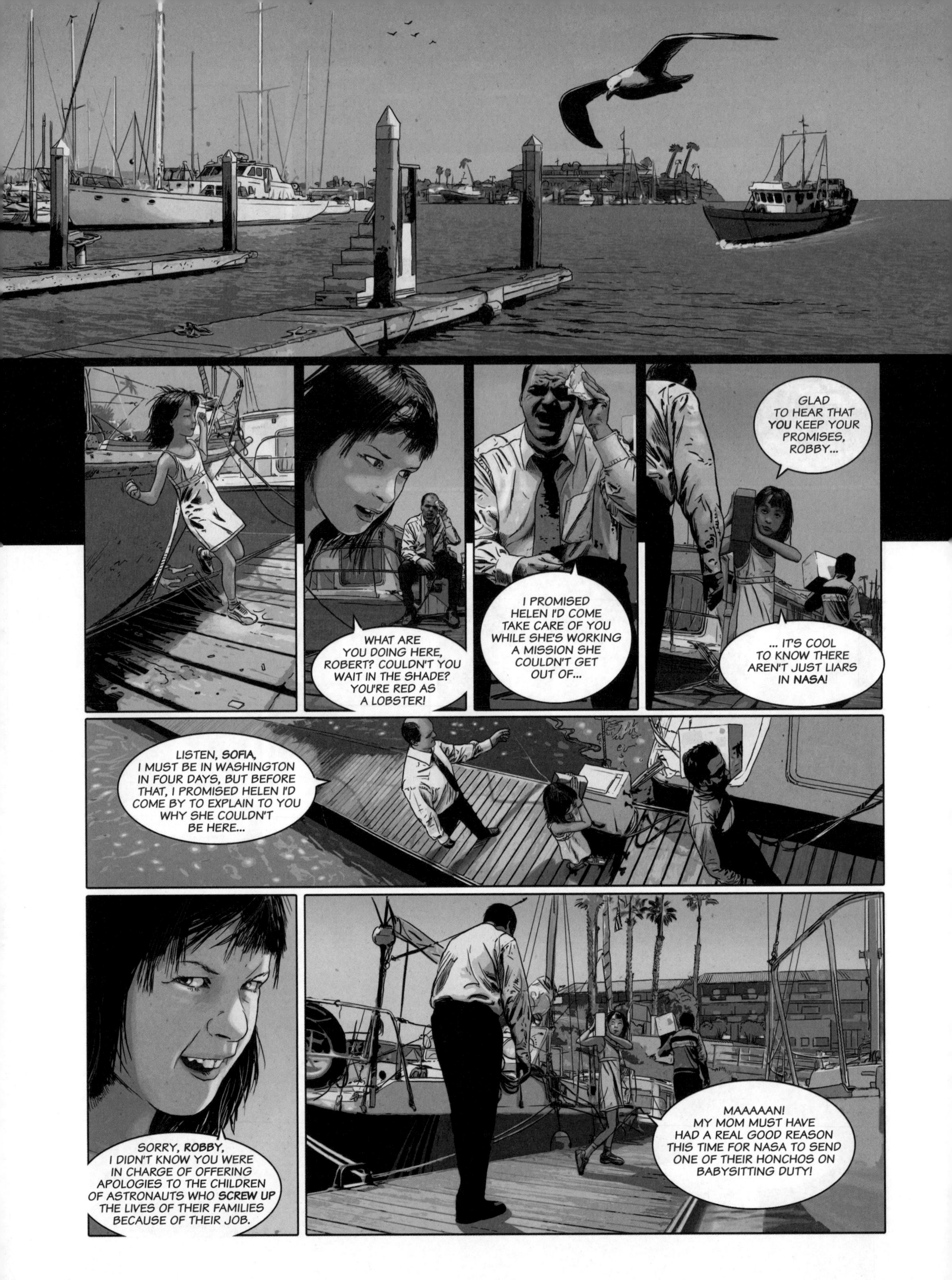
WHAT ARE YOU DOING HERE, ROBERT? COULDN'T YOU WAIT IN THE SHADE? YOU'RE RED AS A LOBSTER!
I PROMISED HELEN I'D COME TAKE CARE OF YOU WHILE SHE'S WORKING A MISSION SHE COULDN'T GET OUT OF...
GLAD TO HEAR THAT YOU KEEP YOUR PROMISES, ROBBY...
... IT'S COOL TO KNOW THERE AREN'T JUST LIARS IN NASA!
LISTEN, SOFIA, I MUST BE IN WASHINGTON IN FOUR DAYS, BUT BEFORE THAT, I PROMISED HELEN I'D COME BY TO EXPLAIN TO YOU WHY SHE COULDN'T BE HERE...
SORRY, ROBBY, I DIDN'T KNOW YOU WERE IN CHARGE OF OFFERING APOLOGIES TO THE CHILDREN OF ASTRONAUTS WHO SCREW UP THE LIVES OF THEIR FAMILIES BECAUSE OF THEIR JOB.
MAAAAAN! MY MOM MUST HAVE HAD A REAL GOOD REASON THIS TIME FOR NASA TO SEND ONE OF THEIR HONCHOS ON BABYSITTING DUTY!

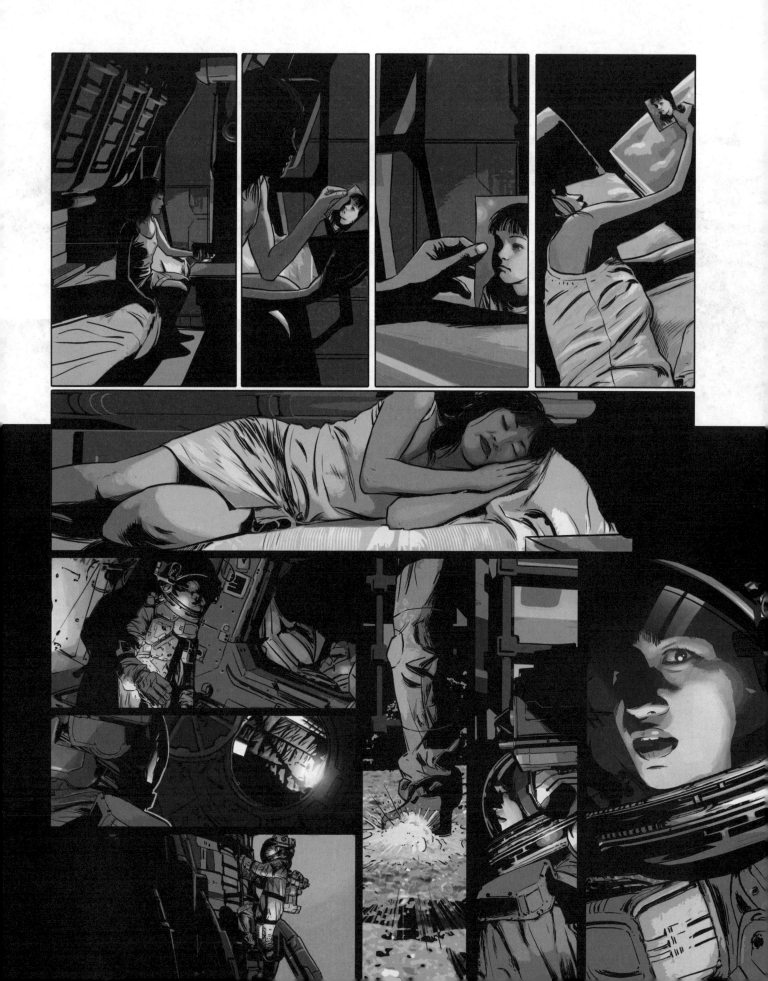

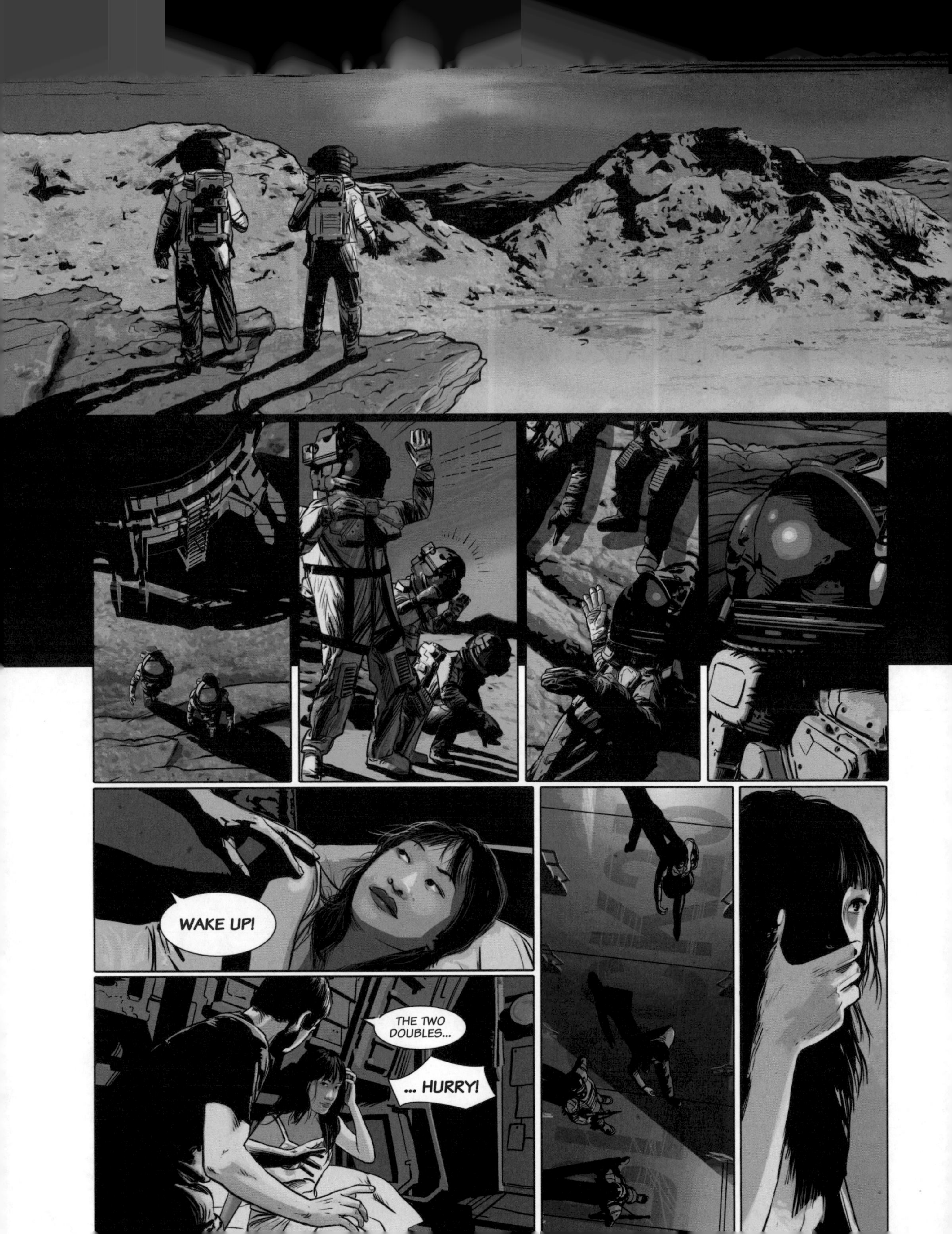
WAKE UP!
THE TWO DOUBLES...
... HURRY!

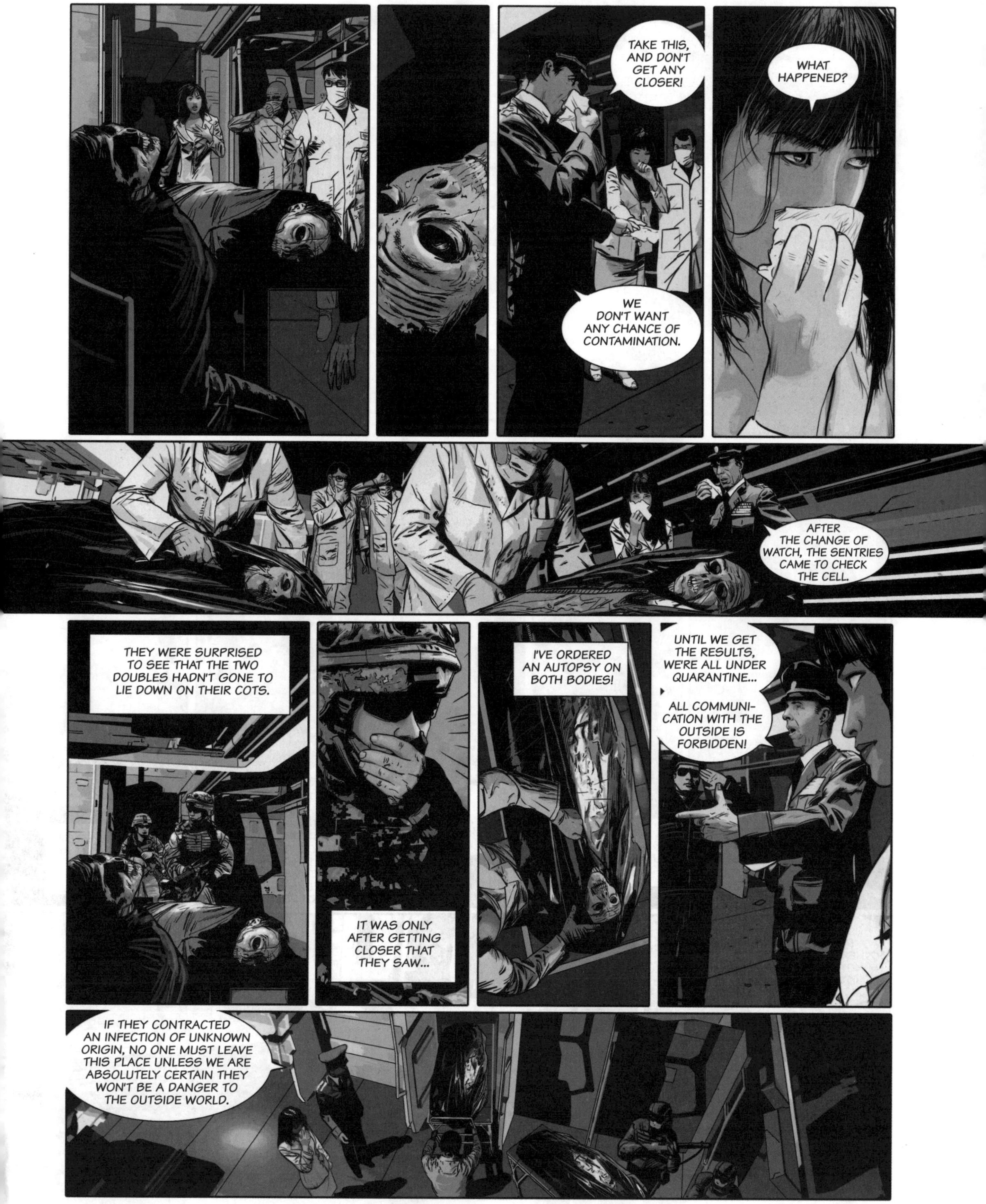

TAKE THIS, AND DON'T GET ANY CLOSER!
WE DON'T WANT ANY CHANCE OF CONTAMINATION.
WHAT HAPPENED?
AFTER THE CHANGE OF WATCH, THE SENTRIES CAME TO CHECK THE CELL.
THEY WERE SURPRISED TO SEE THAT THE TWO DOUBLES HADN'T GONE TO LIE DOWN ON THEIR COTS.
IT WAS ONLY AFTER GETTING CLOSER THAT THEY SAW...
I'VE ORDERED AN AUTOPSY ON BOTH BODIES!
UNTIL WE GET THE RESULTS, WE'RE ALL UNDER QUARANTINE...
ALL COMMUNI-CATION WITH THE OUTSIDE IS FORBIDDEN!
IF THEY CONTRACTED AN INFECTION OF UNKNOWN ORIGIN, NO ONE MUST LEAVE THIS PLACE UNLESS WE ARE ABSOLUTELY CERTAIN THEY WON'T BE A DANGER TO THE OUTSIDE WORLD.

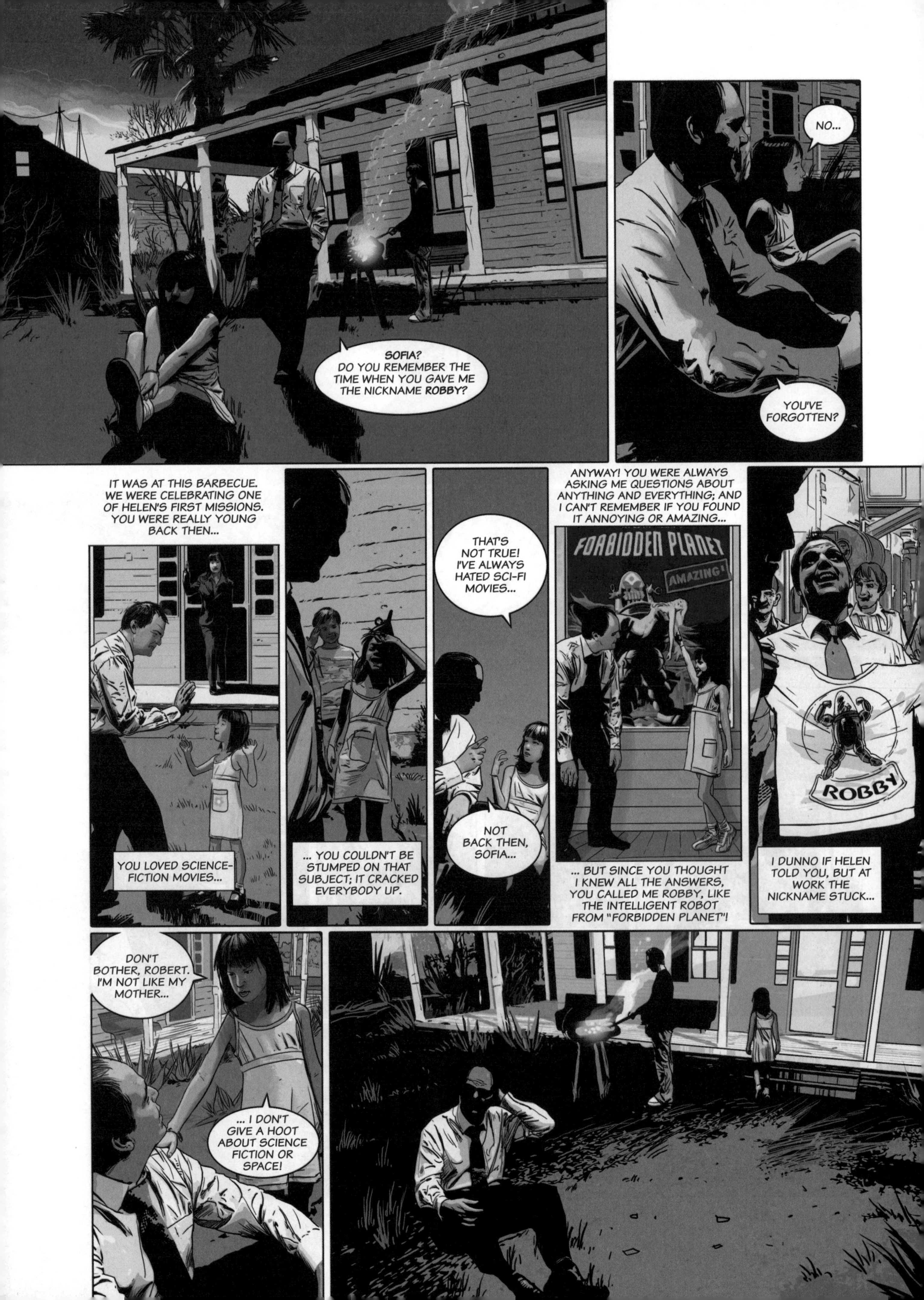
SOFIA? DO YOU REMEMBER THE TIME WHEN YOU GAVE ME THE NICKNAME ROBBY?
NO...
YOU'VE FORGOTTEN?
IT WAS AT THIS BARBECUE. WE WERE CELEBRATING ONE OF HELEN'S FIRST MISSIONS. YOU WERE REALLY YOUNG BACK THEN...
YOU LOVED SCIENCE-FICTION MOVIES...
... YOU COULDN'T BE STUMPED ON THAT SUBJECT; IT CRACKED EVERYBODY UP.
THAT'S NOT TRUE! I'VE ALWAYS HATED SCI-FI MOVIES...
NOT BACK THEN, SOFIA...
ANYWAY! YOU WERE ALWAYS ASKING ME QUESTIONS ABOUT ANYTHING AND EVERYTHING; AND I CAN'T REMEMBER IF YOU FOUND IT ANNOYING OR AMAZING...
FORBIDDEN PLANET
AMAZING!
... BUT SINCE YOU THOUGHT I KNEW ALL THE ANSWERS, YOU CALLED ME ROBBY, LIKE THE INTELLIGENT ROBOT FROM "FORBIDDEN PLANET"!
ROBBY
I DUNNO IF HELEN TOLD YOU, BUT AT WORK THE NICKNAME STUCK...
DON'T BOTHER, ROBERT. I'M NOT LIKE MY MOTHER...
... I DON'T GIVE A HOOT ABOUT SCIENCE FICTION OR SPACE!

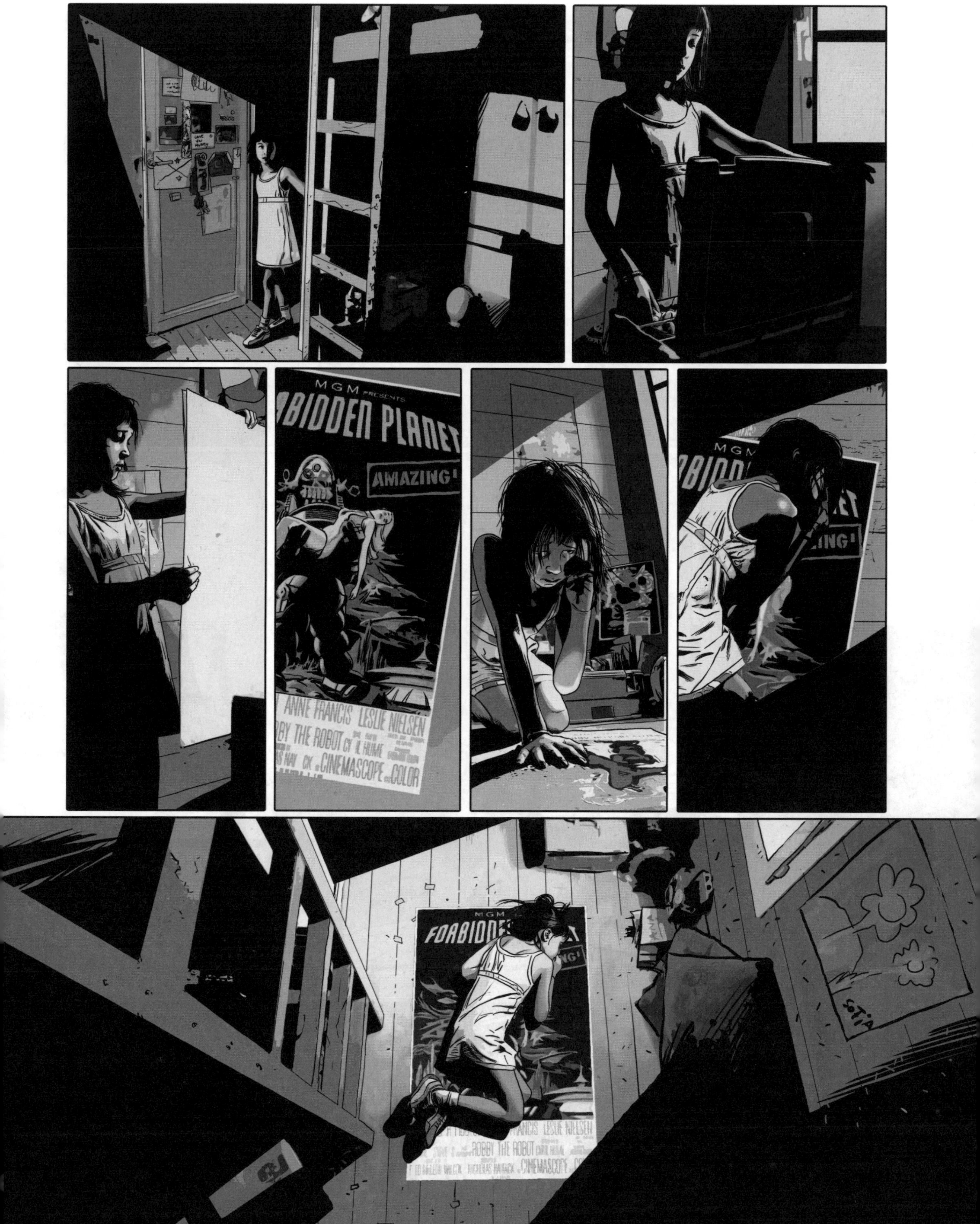
MGM PRESENTS
BIDDEN PLANET
AMAZING!
ANNE FRANCIS LESLIE NIELSEN
CINEMASCOPE
COLOR
FORBIDDEN
ROBBY THE ROBOT

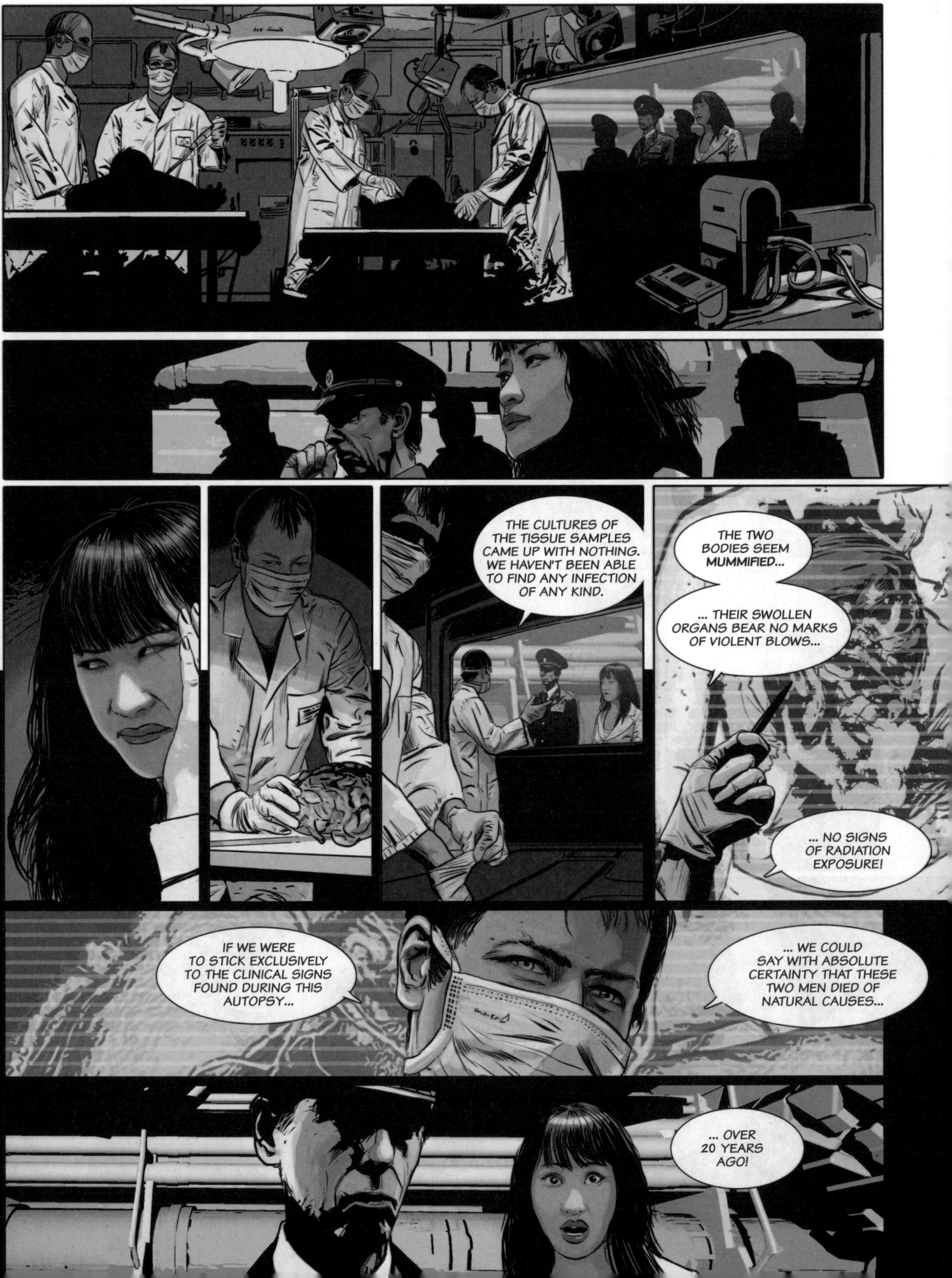
THE CULTURES OF THE TISSUE SAMPLES CAME UP WITH NOTHING. WE HAVEN'T BEEN ABLE TO FIND ANY INFECTION OF ANY KIND.
THE TWO BODIES SEEM MUMMIFIED...
... THEIR SWOLLEN ORGANS BEAR NO MARKS OF VIOLENT BLOWS...
... NO SIGNS OF RADIATION EXPOSURE!
IF WE WERE TO STICK EXCLUSIVELY TO THE CLINICAL SIGNS FOUND DURING THIS AUTOPSY...
... WE COULD SAY WITH ABSOLUTE CERTAINTY THAT THESE TWO MEN DIED OF NATURAL CAUSES...
... OVER 20 YEARS AGO!

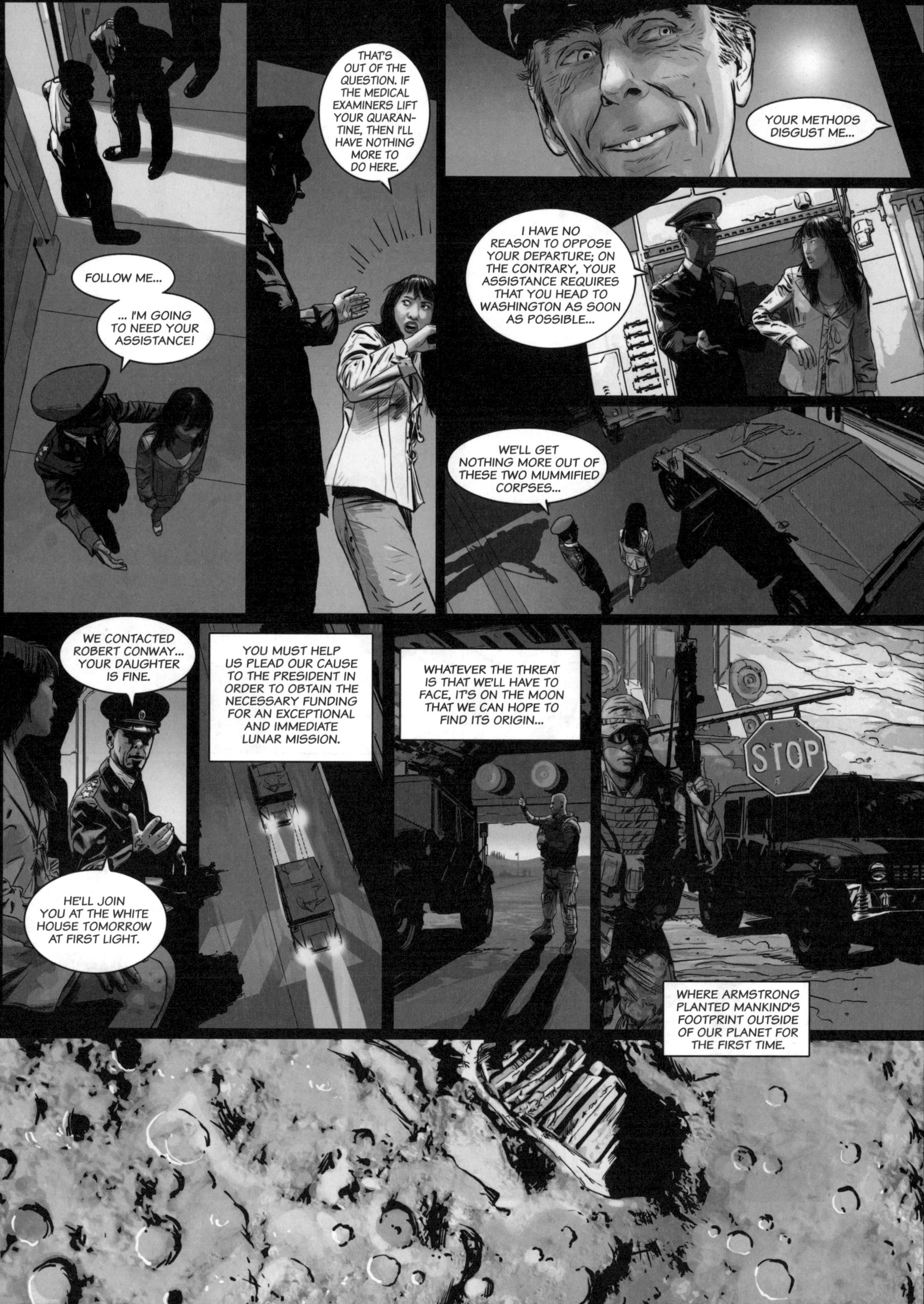
THAT'S OUT OF THE QUESTION. IF THE MEDICAL EXAMINERS LIFT YOUR QUARAN-TINE, THEN I'LL HAVE NOTHING MORE TO DO HERE.
FOLLOW ME...
... I'M GOING TO NEED YOUR ASSISTANCE!
YOUR METHODS DISGUST ME...
I HAVE NO REASON TO OPPOSE YOUR DEPARTURE; ON THE CONTRARY, YOUR ASSISTANCE REQUIRES THAT YOU HEAD TO WASHINGTON AS SOON AS POSSIBLE...
WE'LL GET NOTHING MORE OUT OF THESE TWO MUMMIFIED CORPSES...
WE CONTACTED ROBERT CONWAY... YOUR DAUGHTER IS FINE.
HE'LL JOIN YOU AT THE WHITE HOUSE TOMORROW AT FIRST LIGHT.
YOU MUST HELP US PLEAD OUR CAUSE TO THE PRESIDENT IN ORDER TO OBTAIN THE NECESSARY FUNDING FOR AN EXCEPTIONAL AND IMMEDIATE LUNAR MISSION.
WHATEVER THE THREAT IS THAT WE'LL HAVE TO FACE, IT'S ON THE MOON THAT WE CAN HOPE TO FIND ITS ORIGIN...
STOP
WHERE ARMSTRONG PLANTED MANKIND'S FOOTPRINT OUTSIDE OF OUR PLANET FOR THE FIRST TIME.

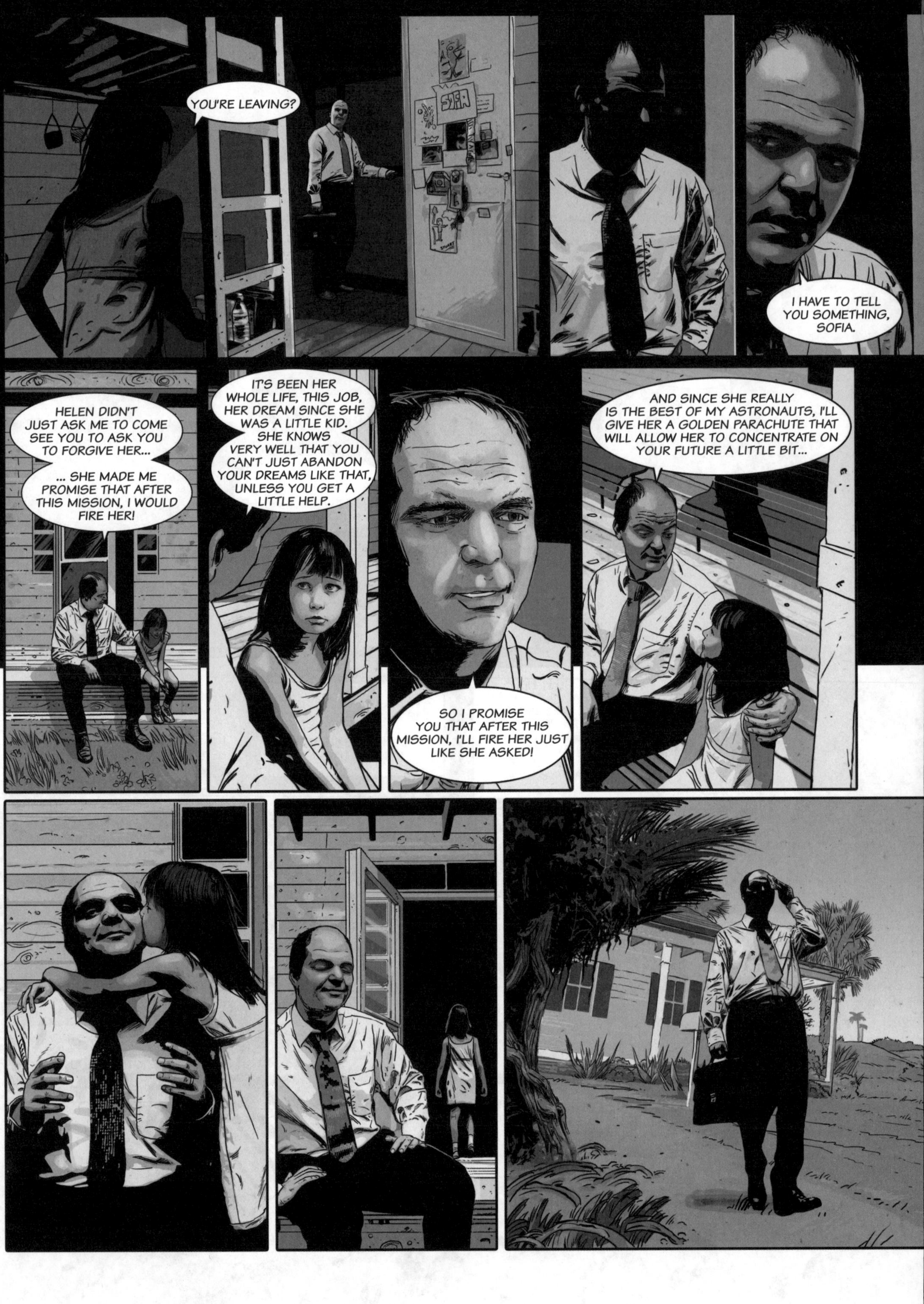
YOU'RE LEAVING?
I HAVE TO TELL YOU SOMETHING, SOFIA.
HELEN DIDN'T JUST ASK ME TO COME SEE YOU TO ASK YOU TO FORGIVE HER...
... SHE MADE ME PROMISE THAT AFTER THIS MISSION, I WOULD FIRE HER!
IT'S BEEN HER WHOLE LIFE, THIS JOB, HER DREAM SINCE SHE WAS A LITTLE KID. SHE KNOWS VERY WELL THAT YOU CAN'T JUST ABANDON YOUR DREAMS LIKE THAT, UNLESS YOU GET A LITTLE HELP.
SO I PROMISE YOU THAT AFTER THIS MISSION, I'LL FIRE HER JUST LIKE SHE ASKED!
AND SINCE SHE REALLY IS THE BEST OF MY ASTRONAUTS, I'LL GIVE HER A GOLDEN PARACHUTE THAT WILL ALLOW HER TO CONCENTRATE ON YOUR FUTURE A LITTLE BIT...

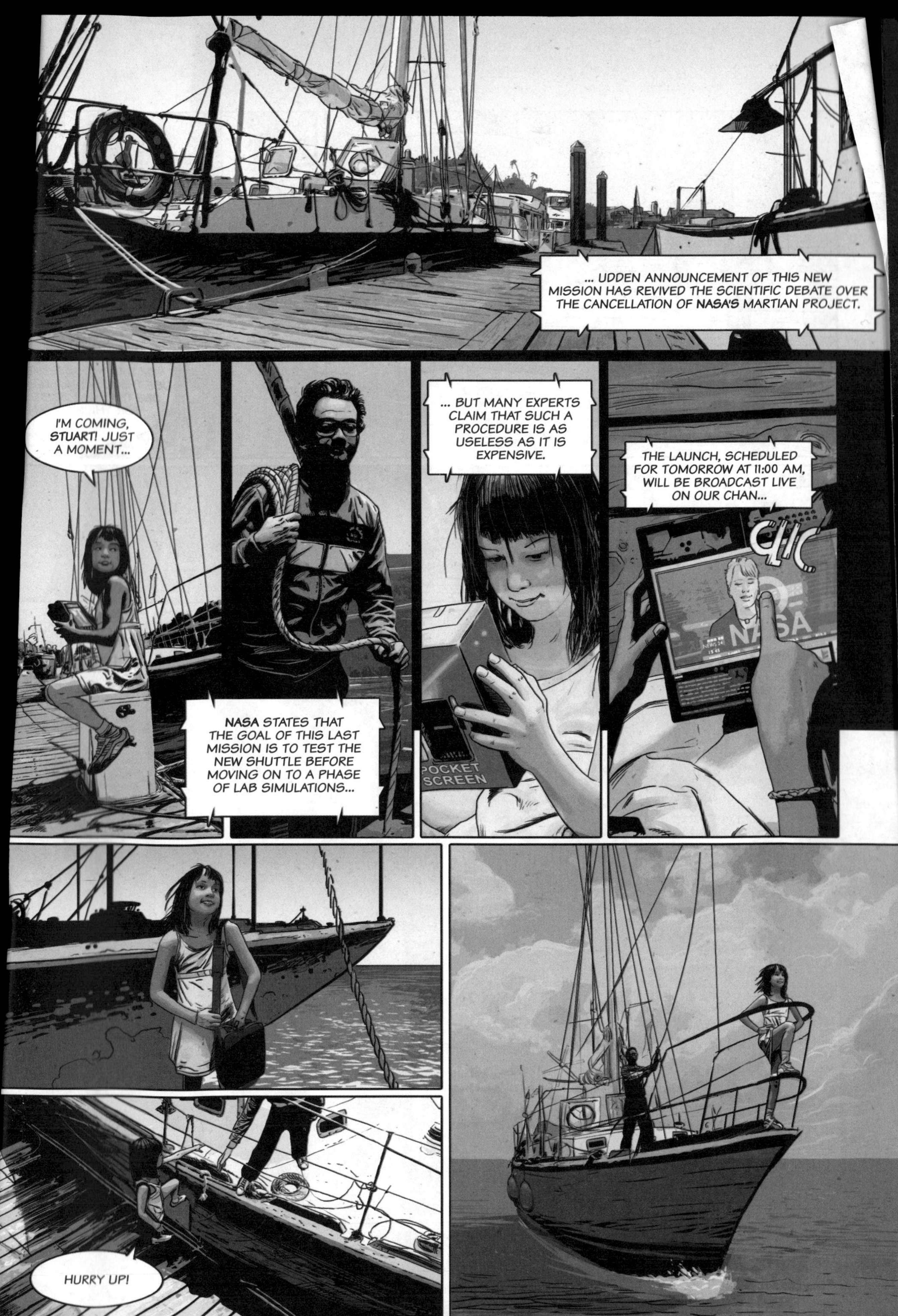
... UDDEN ANNOUNCEMENT OF THIS NEW MISSION HAS REVIVED THE SCIENTIFIC DEBATE OVER THE CANCELLATION OF NASA'S MARTIAN PROJECT.
I'M COMING, STUART! JUST A MOMENT...
NASA STATES THAT THE GOAL OF THIS LAST MISSION IS TO TEST THE NEW SHUTTLE BEFORE MOVING ON TO A PHASE OF LAB SIMULATIONS...
... BUT MANY EXPERTS CLAIM THAT SUCH A PROCEDURE IS AS USELESS AS IT IS EXPENSIVE.
POCKET SCREEN
THE LAUNCH, SCHEDULED FOR TOMORROW AT 11:00 AM, WILL BE BROADCAST LIVE ON OUR CHAN...
NASA
HURRY UP!

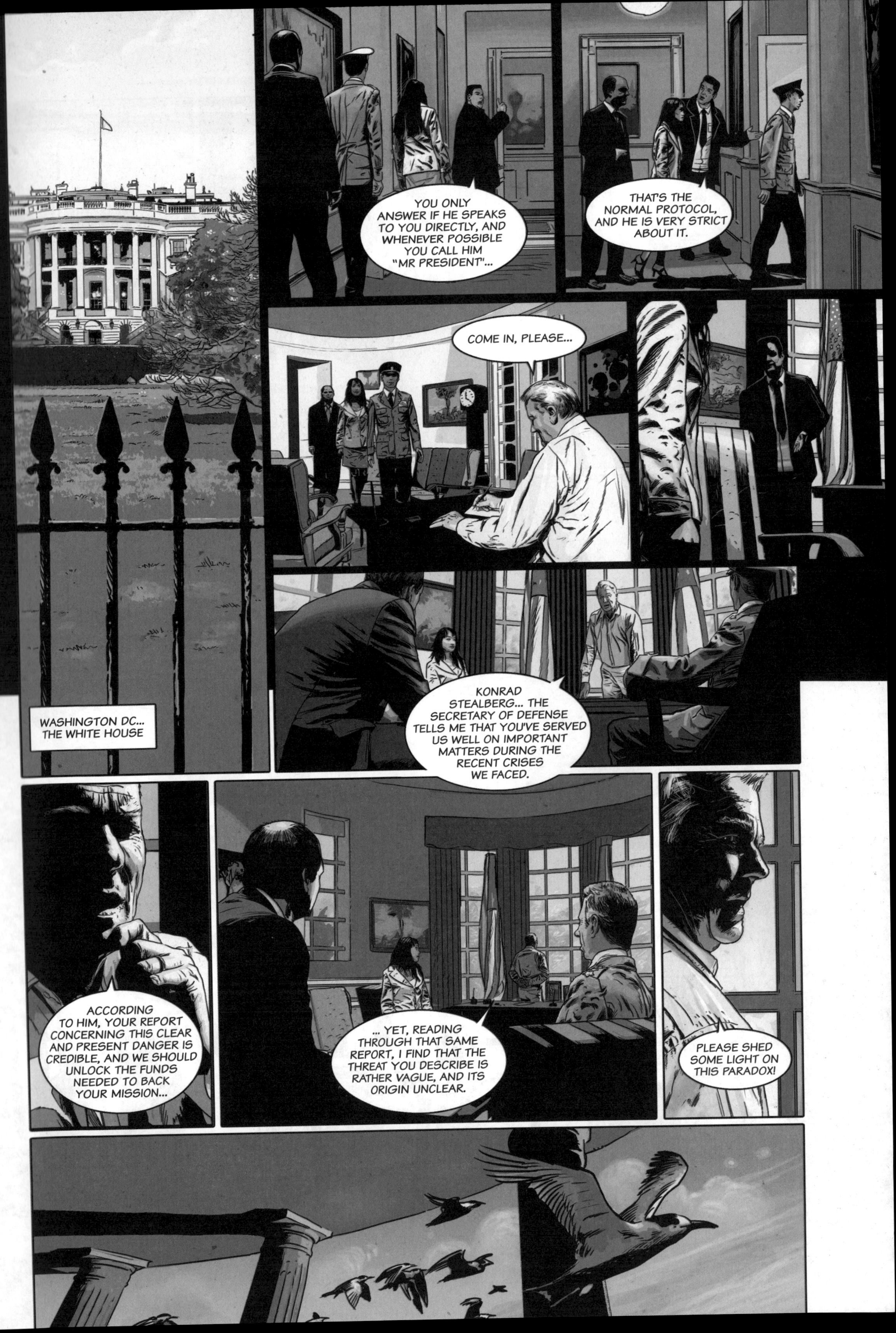
WASHINGTON DC... THE WHITE HOUSE
YOU ONLY ANSWER IF HE SPEAKS TO YOU DIRECTLY, AND WHENEVER POSSIBLE YOU CALL HIM "MR PRESIDENT"...
THAT'S THE NORMAL PROTOCOL, AND HE IS VERY STRICT ABOUT IT.
COME IN, PLEASE...
KONRAD STEALBERG... THE SECRETARY OF DEFENSE TELLS ME THAT YOU'VE SERVED US WELL ON IMPORTANT MATTERS DURING THE RECENT CRISES WE FACED.
ACCORDING TO HIM, YOUR REPORT CONCERNING THIS CLEAR AND PRESENT DANGER IS CREDIBLE, AND WE SHOULD UNLOCK THE FUNDS NEEDED TO BACK YOUR MISSION...
... YET, READING THROUGH THAT SAME REPORT, I FIND THAT THE THREAT YOU DESCRIBE IS RATHER VAGUE, AND ITS ORIGIN UNCLEAR.
PLEASE SHED SOME LIGHT ON THIS PARADOX!

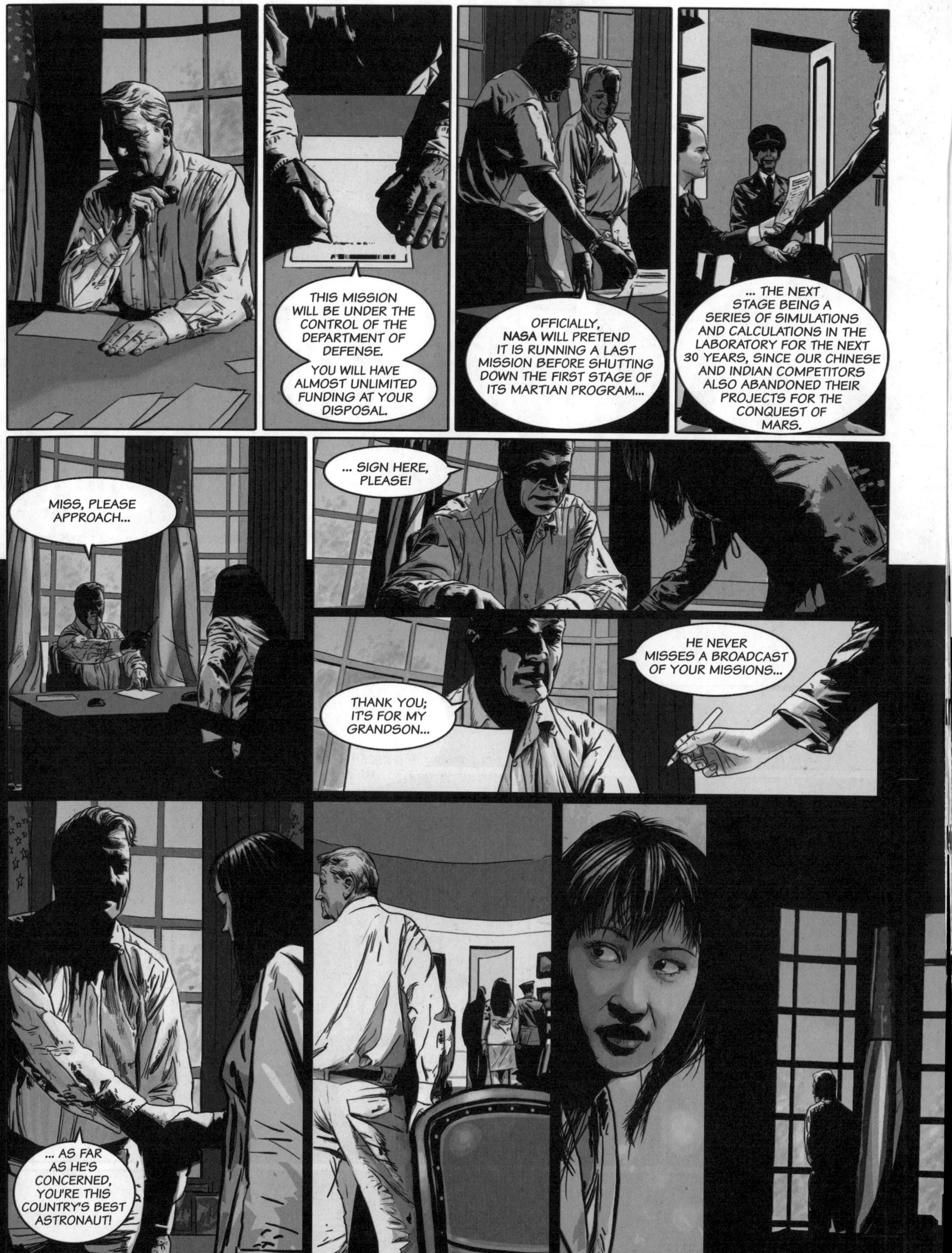
THIS MISSION WILL BE UNDER THE CONTROL OF THE DEPARTMENT OF DEFENSE.
YOU WILL HAVE ALMOST UNLIMITED FUNDING AT YOUR DISPOSAL.
OFFICIALLY, NASA WILL PRETEND IT IS RUNNING A LAST MISSION BEFORE SHUTTING DOWN THE FIRST STAGE OF ITS MARTIAN PROGRAM...
... THE NEXT STAGE BEING A SERIES OF SIMULATIONS AND CALCULATIONS IN THE LABORATORY FOR THE NEXT 30 YEARS, SINCE OUR CHINESE AND INDIAN COMPETITORS ALSO ABANDONED THEIR PROJECTS FOR THE CONQUEST OF MARS.
MISS, PLEASE APPROACH...
... SIGN HERE, PLEASE!
THANK YOU; IT'S FOR MY GRANDSON...
HE NEVER MISSES A BROADCAST OF YOUR MISSIONS...
... AS FAR AS HE'S CONCERNED, YOU'RE THIS COUNTRY'S BEST ASTRONAUT!

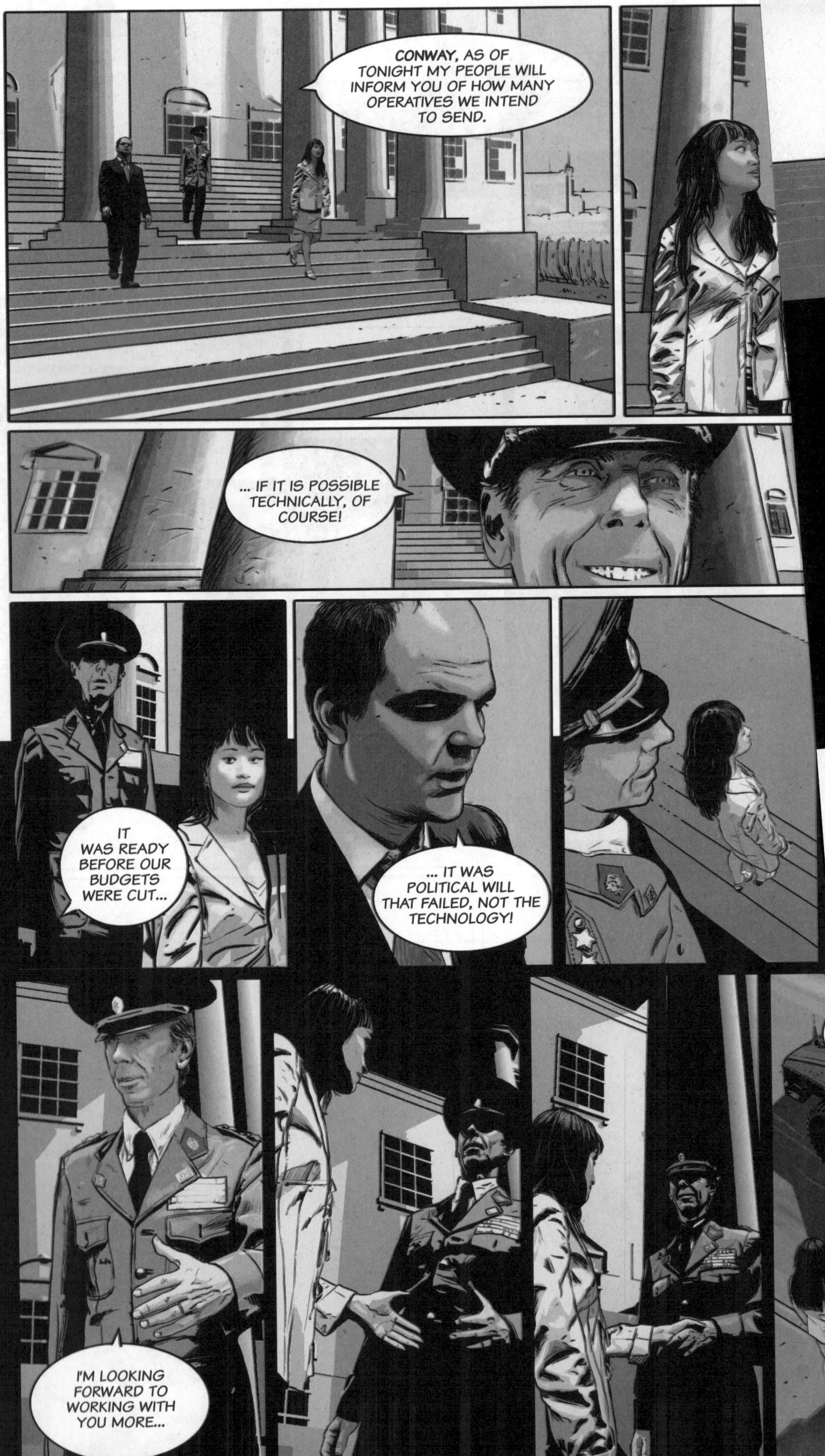
CONWAY, AS OF TONIGHT MY PEOPLE WILL INFORM YOU OF HOW MANY OPERATIVES WE INTEND TO SEND.
... IF IT IS POSSIBLE TECHNICALLY, OF COURSE!
IT WAS READY BEFORE OUR BUDGETS WERE CUT...
... IT WAS POLITICAL WILL THAT FAILED, NOT THE TECHNOLOGY!
I'M LOOKING FORWARD TO WORKING WITH YOU MORE...

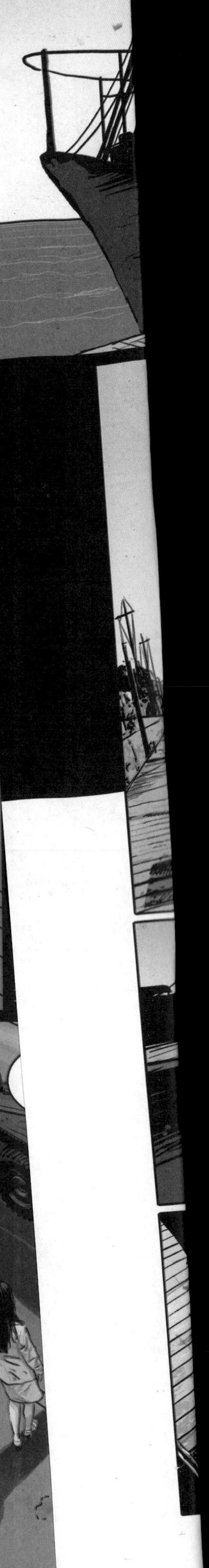

CAPE CANAVERAL

THIS ISN'T JUST ANOTHER MISSION. YOU'RE NOT TELLING US EVERYTHING, HELEN!

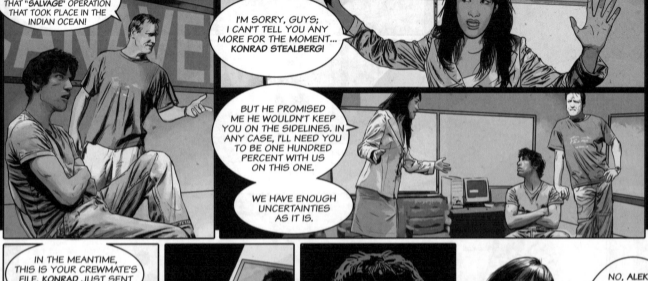

YEAH, AND WE HEARD IT'S GOT SOMETHING TO DO WITH THAT "SALVAGE" OPERATION THAT TOOK PLACE IN THE INDIAN OCEAN!

I'M SORRY, GUYS; I CAN'T TELL YOU ANY MORE FOR THE MOMENT... KONRAD STEALBERG!

BUT HE PROMISED ME HE WOULDN'T KEEP YOU ON THE SIDELINES. IN ANY CASE, I'LL NEED YOU TO BE ONE HUNDRED PERCENT WITH US ON THIS ONE.

WE HAVE ENOUGH UNCERTAINTIES AS IT IS.

IN THE MEANTIME, THIS IS YOUR CREWMATE'S FILE. KONRAD JUST SENT IT TO ME TODAY.

OBVIOUSLY HIS DEPARTMENT HAD MORE TROUBLE MAKING THEIR CHOICE THAN WE DID.

ALEXANDRA CALDERON, IN HER THIRTIES, FORMER MARINE. SAW ACTION IN PAKISTAN AND INDONESIA, THEN CHANGED CAREERS AND BECAME AN ENGINEER.

HANG ON! DON'T TELL ME YOU'RE TAKING THE CONTENT OF THIS FILE AT FACE VALUE. THESE GUYS WORK FOR THE CIA, OBVIOUSLY. PERSONNEL FILES CAN BE TWEAKED ANY WAY THEY WANT.

NO, ALEKSA, THEY DON'T WORK FOR THE CIA. I CHECKED; WE HAVE AN INTELLIGENCE SECTION TOO, YOU KNOW... BUT I DON'T GIVE A DAMN WHAT AGENCY THEY WORK FOR. FOR THE MOMENT, WE'LL GO WITH WHAT STEALBERG TELLS US.

HELEN, MEETING IN ROBBY'S OFFICE IN FIVE MINUTES. STEALBERG HAS ARRIVED.

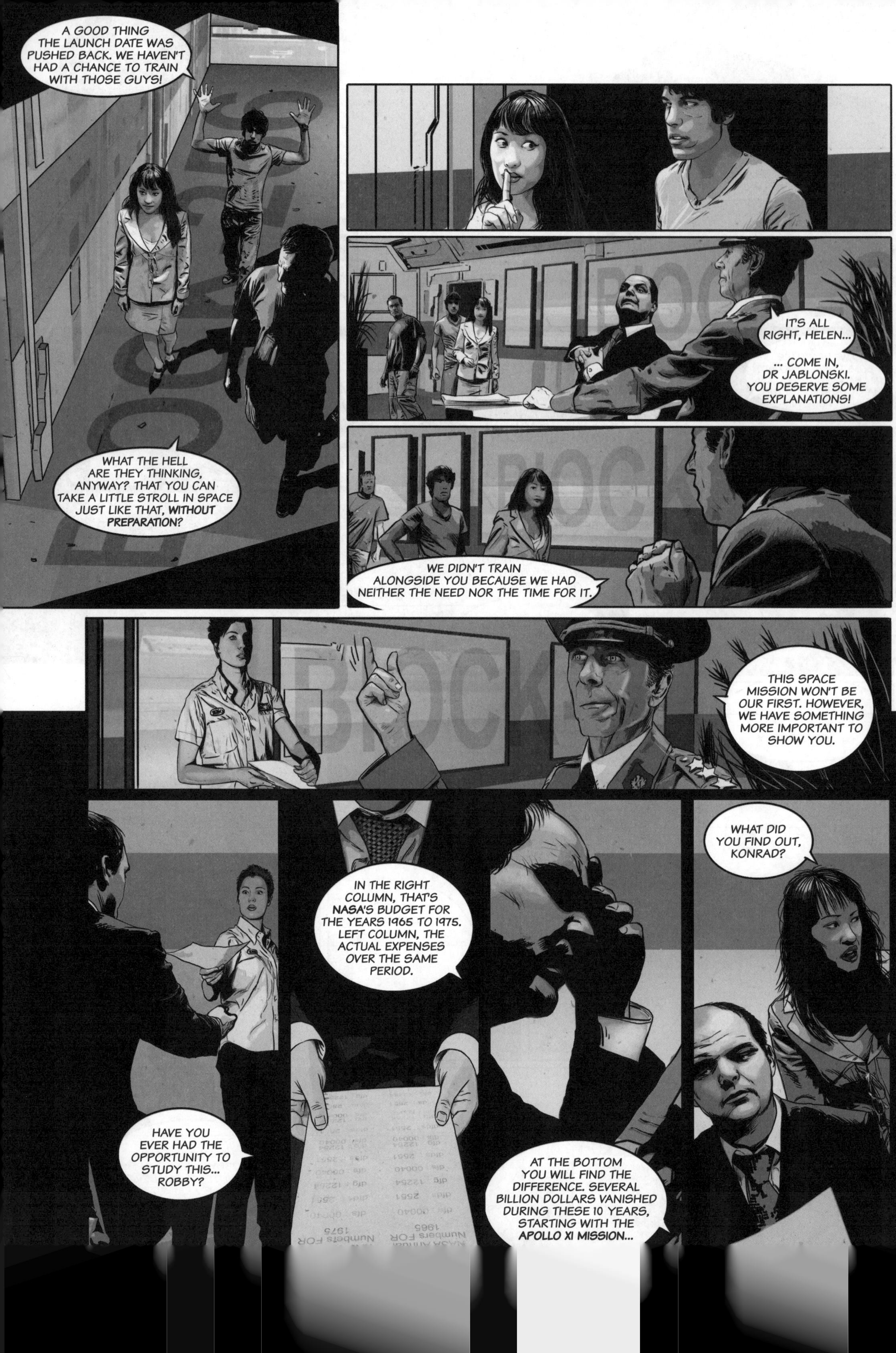
A GOOD THING THE LAUNCH DATE WAS PUSHED BACK. WE HAVEN'T HAD A CHANCE TO TRAIN WITH THOSE GUYS!
WHAT THE HELL ARE THEY THINKING, ANYWAY? THAT YOU CAN TAKE A LITTLE STROLL IN SPACE JUST LIKE THAT, WITHOUT PREPARATION?
IT'S ALL RIGHT, HELEN...
... COME IN, DR JABLONSKI. YOU DESERVE SOME EXPLANATIONS!
WE DIDN'T TRAIN ALONGSIDE YOU BECAUSE WE HAD NEITHER THE NEED NOR THE TIME FOR IT.
THIS SPACE MISSION WON'T BE OUR FIRST. HOWEVER, WE HAVE SOMETHING MORE IMPORTANT TO SHOW YOU.
HAVE YOU EVER HAD THE OPPORTUNITY TO STUDY THIS... ROBBY?
IN THE RIGHT COLUMN, THAT'S NASA'S BUDGET FOR THE YEARS 1965 TO 1975. LEFT COLUMN, THE ACTUAL EXPENSES OVER THE SAME PERIOD.
AT THE BOTTOM YOU WILL FIND THE DIFFERENCE. SEVERAL BILLION DOLLARS VANISHED DURING THESE 10 YEARS, STARTING WITH THE APOLLO XI MISSION...
WHAT DID YOU FIND OUT, KONRAD?

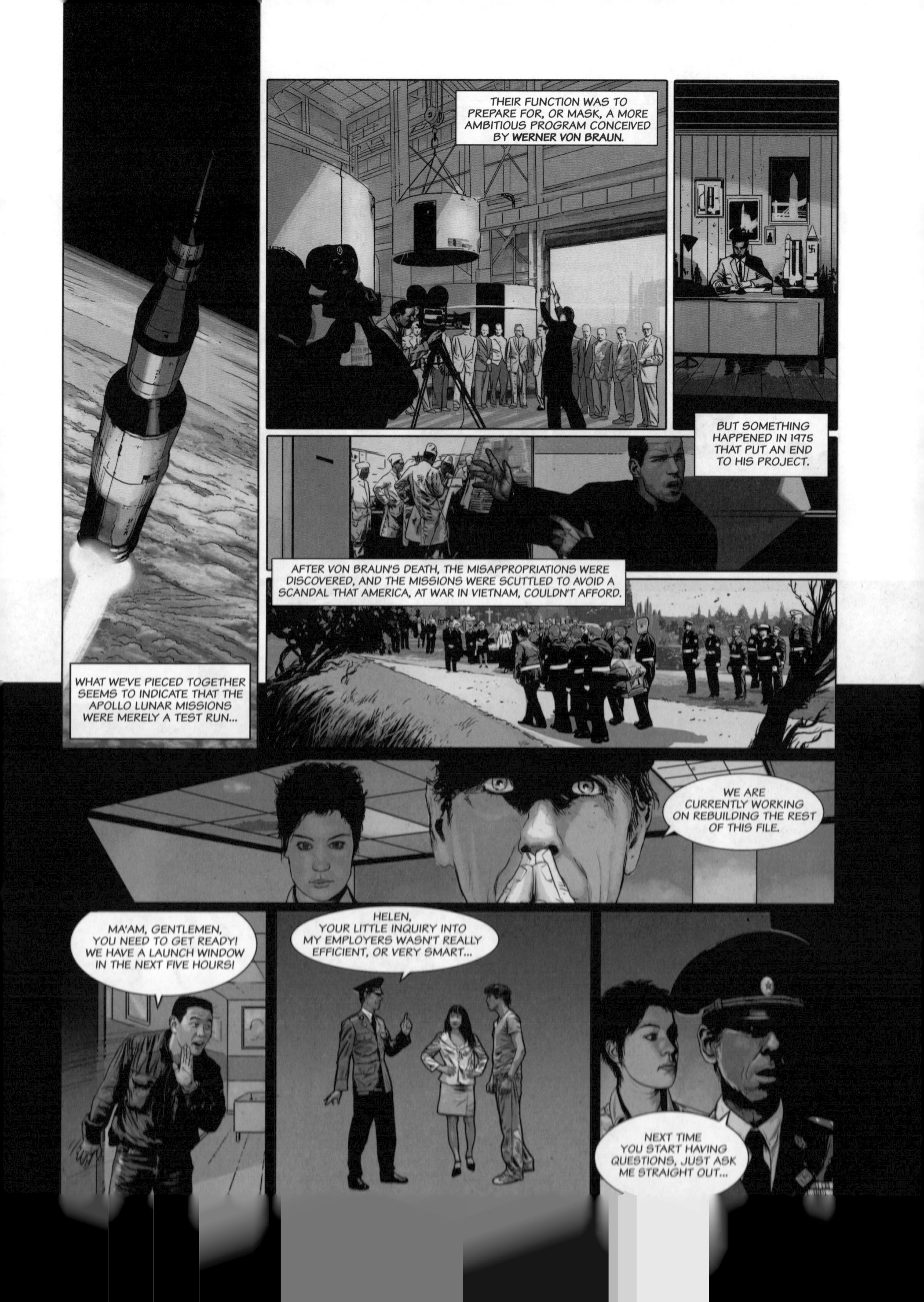
WHAT WE'VE PIECED TOGETHER SEEMS TO INDICATE THAT THE APOLLO LUNAR MISSIONS WERE MERELY A TEST RUN...
THEIR FUNCTION WAS TO PREPARE FOR, OR MASK, A MORE AMBITIOUS PROGRAM CONCEIVED BY WERNER VON BRAUN.
BUT SOMETHING HAPPENED IN 1975 THAT PUT AN END TO HIS PROJECT.
AFTER VON BRAUN'S DEATH, THE MISAPPROPRIATIONS WERE DISCOVERED, AND THE MISSIONS WERE SCUTTLED TO AVOID A SCANDAL THAT AMERICA, AT WAR IN VIETNAM, COULDN'T AFFORD.
WE ARE CURRENTLY WORKING ON REBUILDING THE REST OF THIS FILE.
MA'AM, GENTLEMEN, YOU NEED TO GET READY! WE HAVE A LAUNCH WINDOW IN THE NEXT FIVE HOURS!
HELEN, YOUR LITTLE INQUIRY INTO MY EMPLOYERS WASN'T REALLY EFFICIENT, OR VERY SMART...
NEXT TIME YOU START HAVING QUESTIONS, JUST ASK ME STRAIGHT OUT...

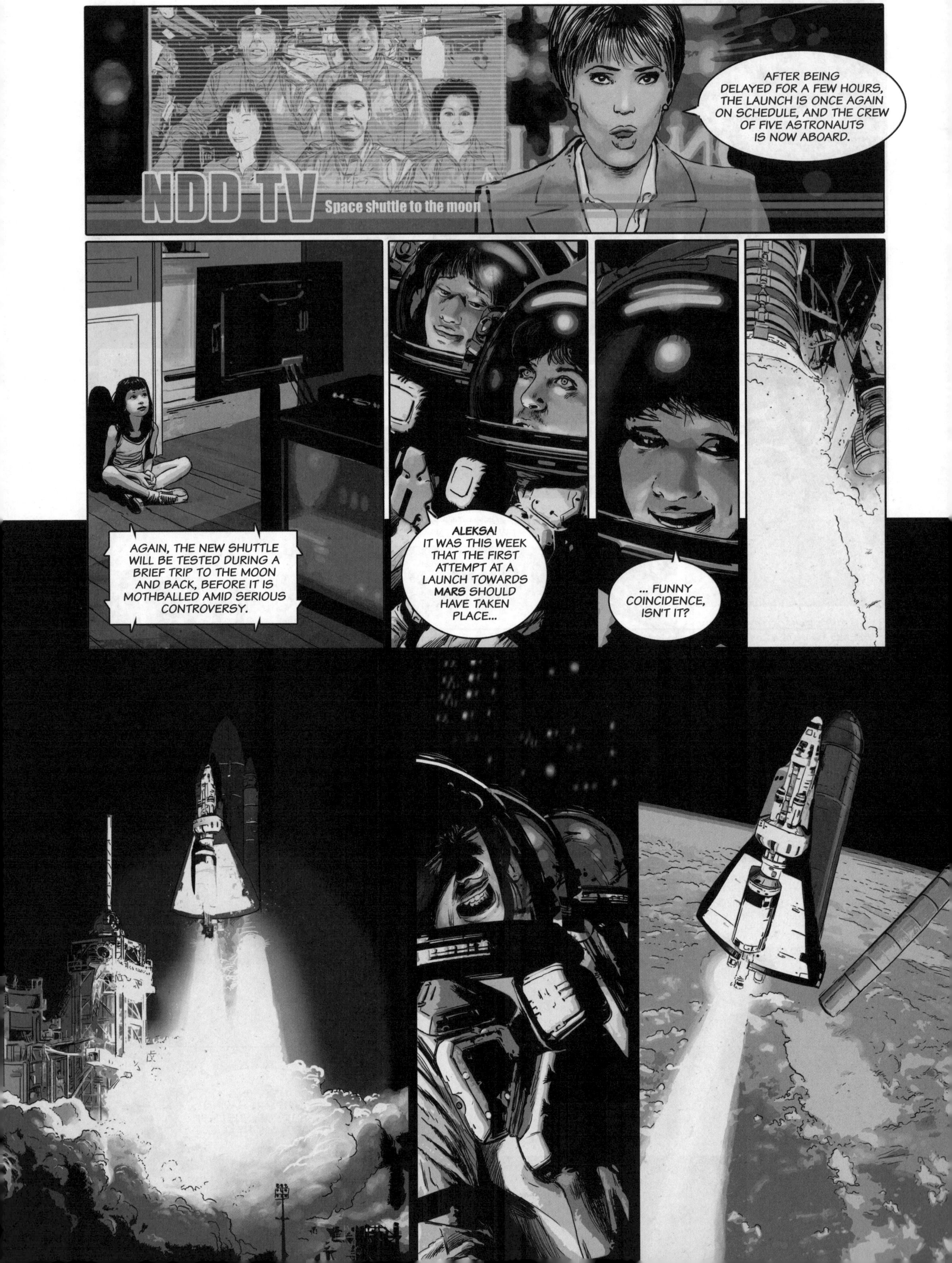
NDD TV
Space shuttle to the moon
AFTER BEING DELAYED FOR A FEW HOURS, THE LAUNCH IS ONCE AGAIN ON SCHEDULE, AND THE CREW OF FIVE ASTRONAUTS IS NOW ABOARD.
AGAIN, THE NEW SHUTTLE WILL BE TESTED DURING A BRIEF TRIP TO THE MOON AND BACK, BEFORE IT IS MOTHBALLED AMID SERIOUS CONTROVERSY.
ALEKSA! IT WAS THIS WEEK THAT THE FIRST ATTEMPT AT A LAUNCH TOWARDS MARS SHOULD HAVE TAKEN PLACE...
... FUNNY COINCIDENCE, ISN'T IT?

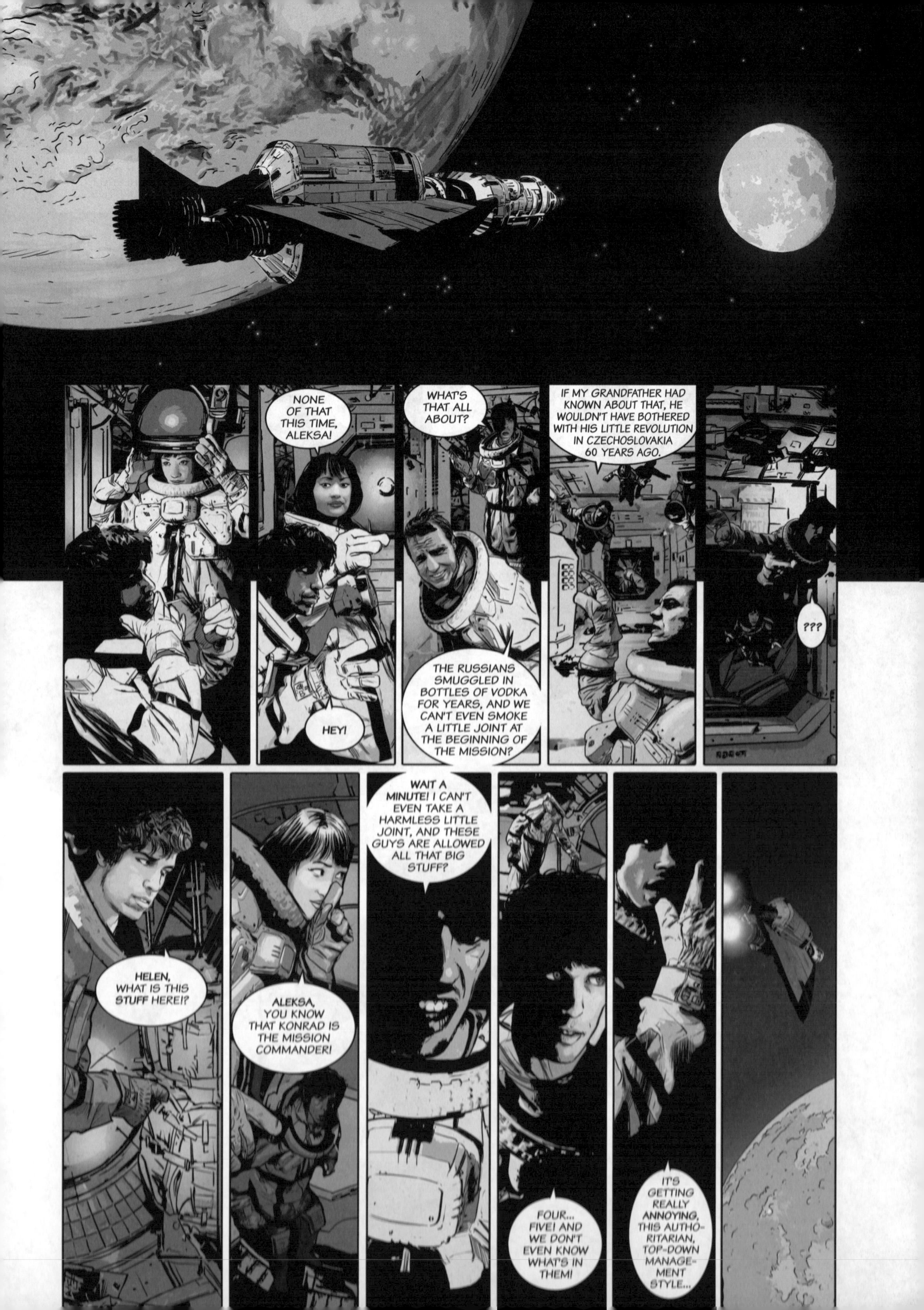

NONE OF THAT THIS TIME, ALEKSA!
HEY!
WHAT'S THAT ALL ABOUT?
THE RUSSIANS SMUGGLED IN BOTTLES OF VODKA FOR YEARS, AND WE CAN'T EVEN SMOKE A LITTLE JOINT AT THE BEGINNING OF THE MISSION?
IF MY GRANDFATHER HAD KNOWN ABOUT THAT, HE WOULDN'T HAVE BOTHERED WITH HIS LITTLE REVOLUTION IN CZECHOSLOVAKIA 60 YEARS AGO.
???
HELEN, WHAT IS THIS STUFF HERE!?
ALEKSA, YOU KNOW THAT KONRAD IS THE MISSION COMMANDER!
WAIT A MINUTE! I CAN'T EVEN TAKE A HARMLESS LITTLE JOINT, AND THESE GUYS ARE ALLOWED ALL THAT BIG STUFF?
FOUR... FIVE! AND WE DON'T EVEN KNOW WHAT'S IN THEM!
IT'S GETTING REALLY ANNOYING, THIS AUTHO-RITARIAN, TOP-DOWN MANAGE-MENT STYLE...

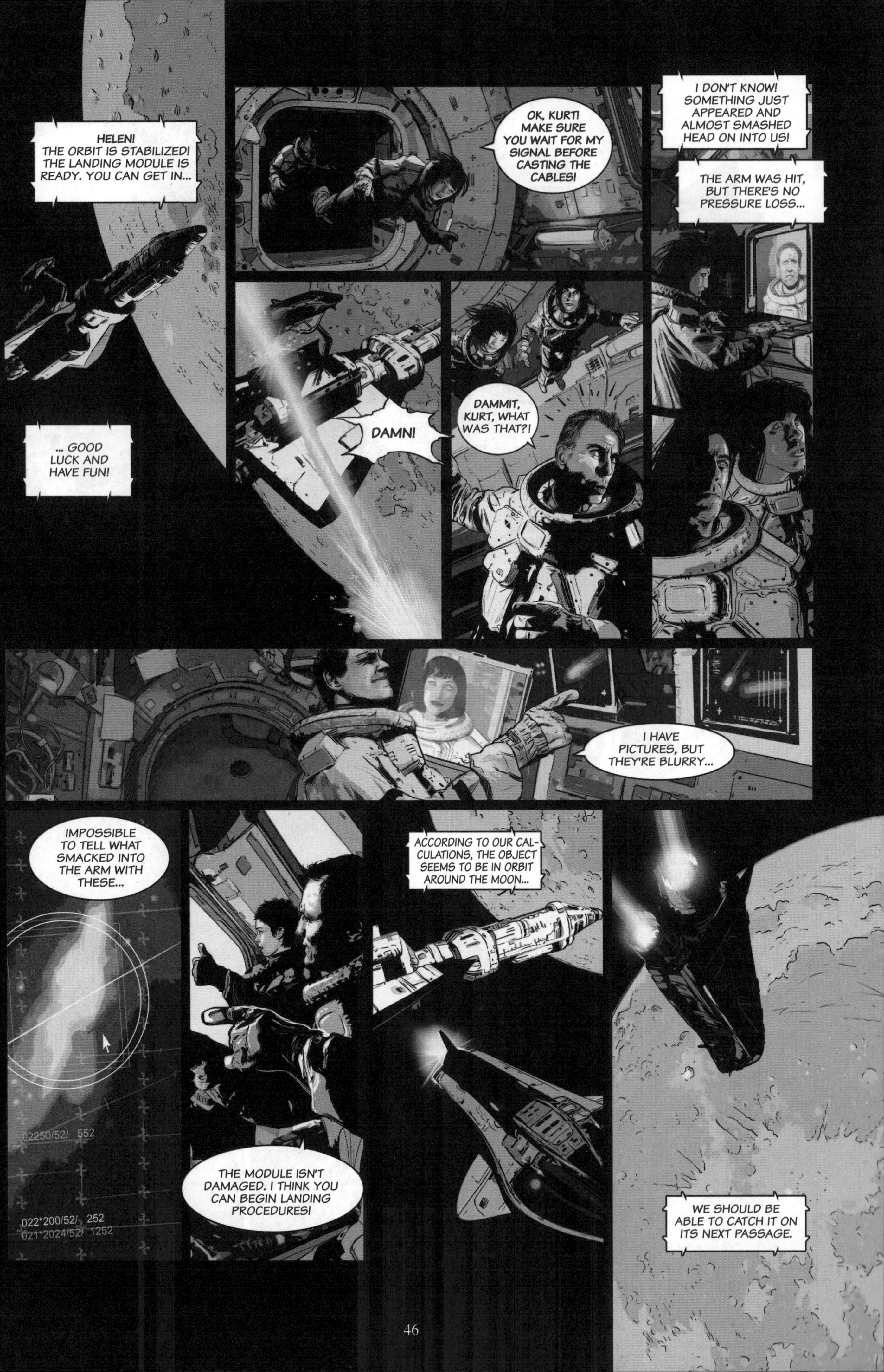
HELEN! THE ORBIT IS STABILIZED! THE LANDING MODULE IS READY. YOU CAN GET IN...
... GOOD LUCK AND HAVE FUN!
OK, KURT! MAKE SURE YOU WAIT FOR MY SIGNAL BEFORE CASTING THE CABLES!
DAMN!
DAMMIT, KURT, WHAT WAS THAT?!
I DON'T KNOW! SOMETHING JUST APPEARED AND ALMOST SMASHED HEAD ON INTO US!
THE ARM WAS HIT, BUT THERE'S NO PRESSURE LOSS...
I HAVE PICTURES, BUT THEY'RE BLURRY...
IMPOSSIBLE TO TELL WHAT SMACKED INTO THE ARM WITH THESE...
02250/52/ 552
022*200/52/ 252
021*2024/52/ 1252
THE MODULE ISN'T DAMAGED. I THINK YOU CAN BEGIN LANDING PROCEDURES!
ACCORDING TO OUR CALCULATIONS, THE OBJECT SEEMS TO BE IN ORBIT AROUND THE MOON...
WE SHOULD BE ABLE TO CATCH IT ON ITS NEXT PASSAGE.

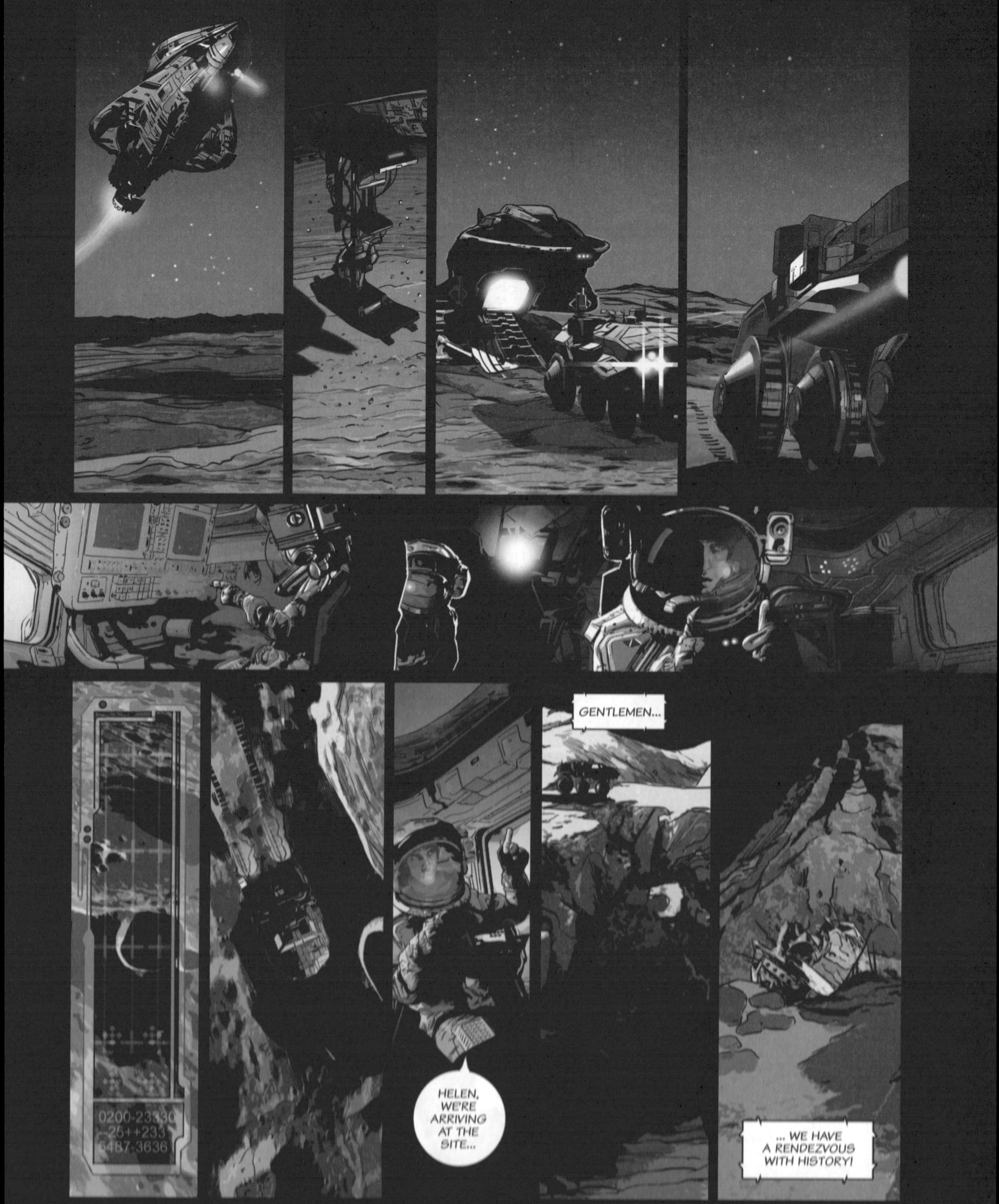
HELEN, WE'RE ARRIVING AT THE SITE...
GENTLEMEN...
... WE HAVE A RENDEZVOUS WITH HISTORY!

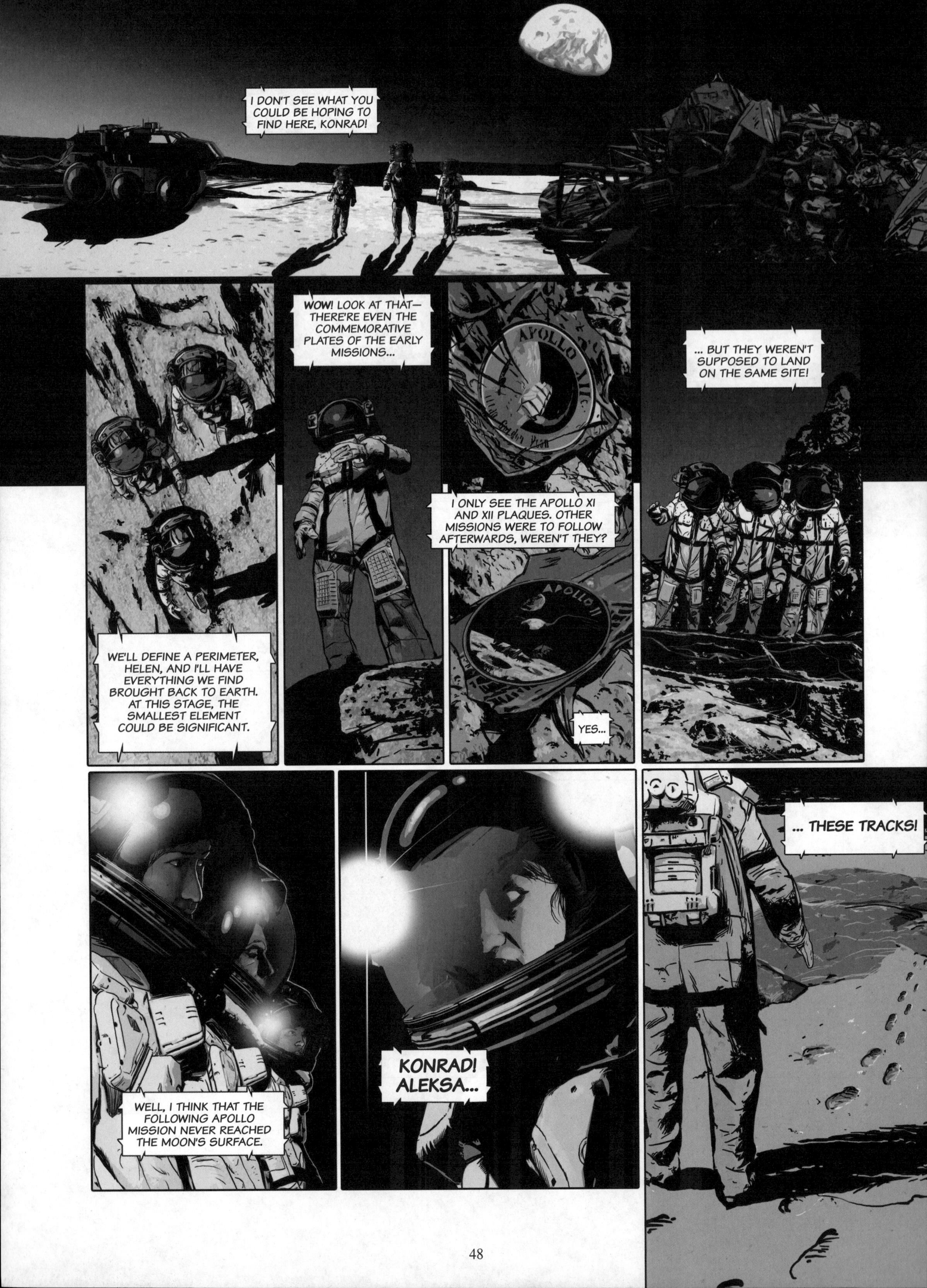
I DON'T SEE WHAT YOU COULD BE HOPING TO FIND HERE, KONRAD!
WE'LL DEFINE A PERIMETER, HELEN, AND I'LL HAVE EVERYTHING WE FIND BROUGHT BACK TO EARTH. AT THIS STAGE, THE SMALLEST ELEMENT COULD BE SIGNIFICANT.
WOW! LOOK AT THAT— THERE'RE EVEN THE COMMEMORATIVE PLATES OF THE EARLY MISSIONS...
APOLLO XII
I ONLY SEE THE APOLLO XI AND XII PLAQUES. OTHER MISSIONS WERE TO FOLLOW AFTERWARDS, WEREN'T THEY?
APOLLO 11
YES...
... BUT THEY WEREN'T SUPPOSED TO LAND ON THE SAME SITE!
WELL, I THINK THAT THE FOLLOWING APOLLO MISSION NEVER REACHED THE MOON'S SURFACE.
KONRAD! ALEKSA...
... THESE TRACKS!

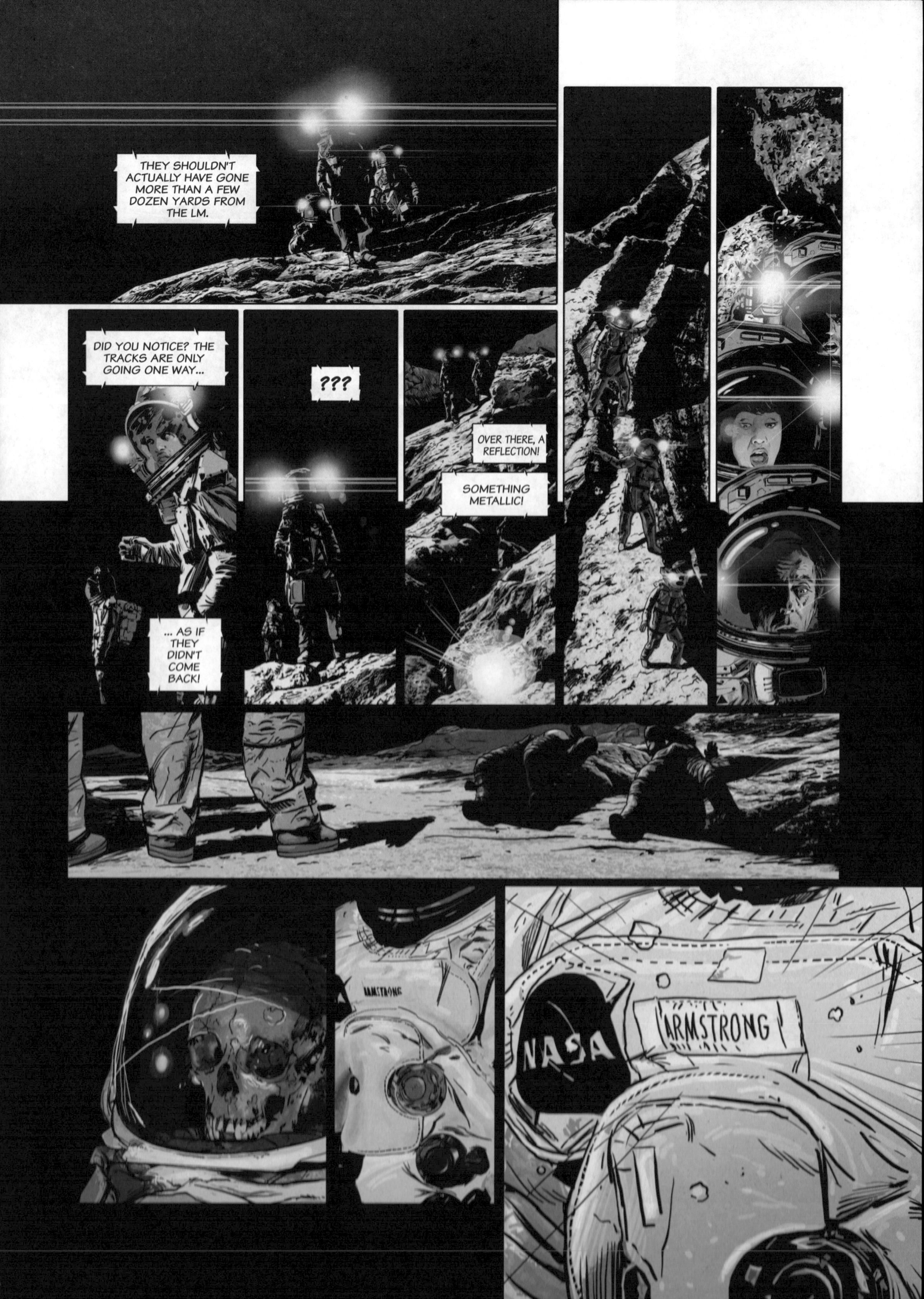
THEY SHOULDN'T ACTUALLY HAVE GONE MORE THAN A FEW DOZEN YARDS FROM THE LM.
DID YOU NOTICE? THE TRACKS ARE ONLY GOING ONE WAY...
... AS IF THEY DIDN'T COME BACK!
???
OVER THERE, A REFLECTION!
SOMETHING METALLIC!
ARMSTRONG
NASA
ARMSTRONG

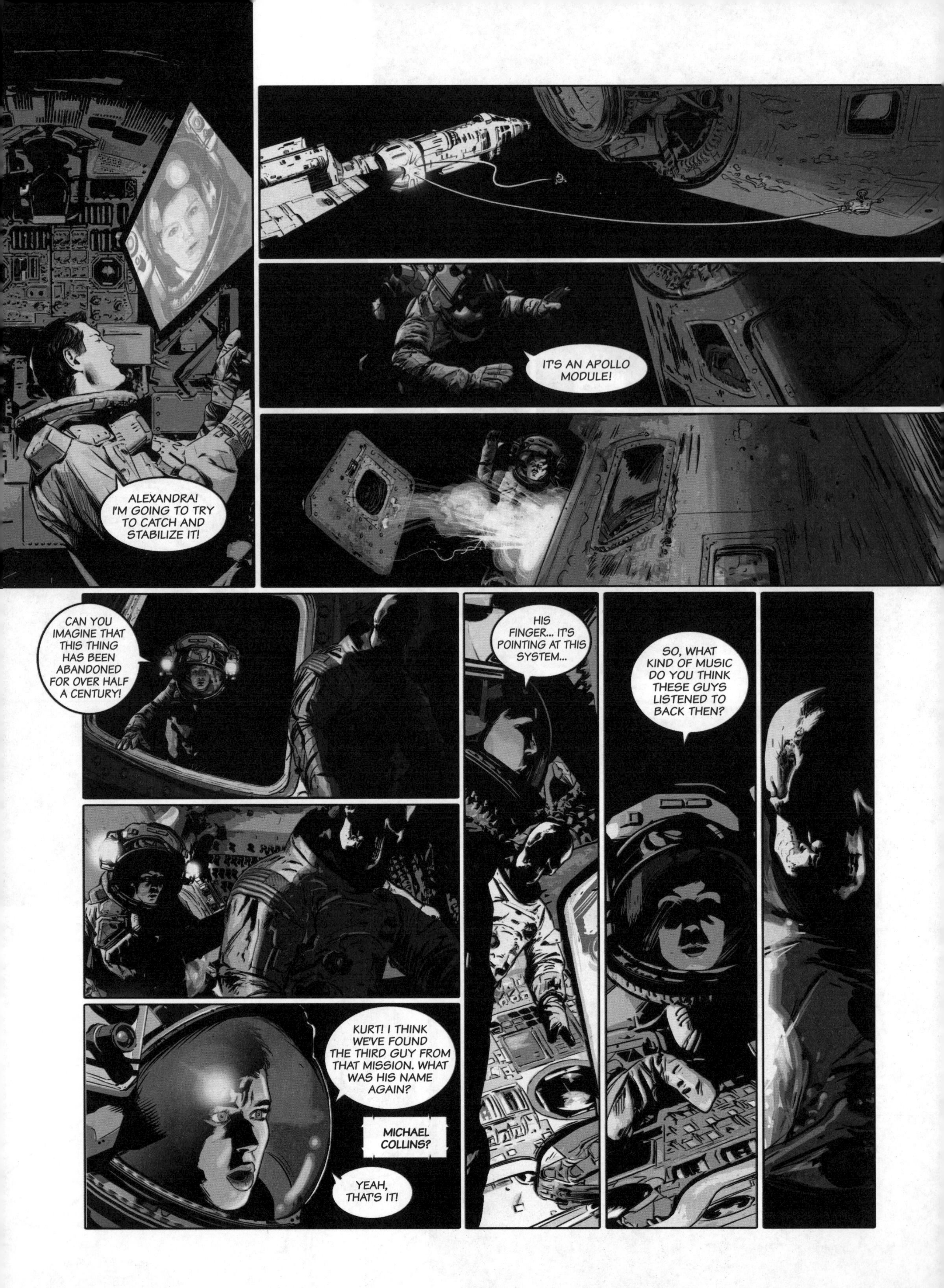
ALEXANDRA! I'M GOING TO TRY TO CATCH AND STABILIZE IT!
IT'S AN APOLLO MODULE!
CAN YOU IMAGINE THAT THIS THING HAS BEEN ABANDONED FOR OVER HALF A CENTURY!
KURT! I THINK WE'VE FOUND THE THIRD GUY FROM THAT MISSION. WHAT WAS HIS NAME AGAIN?
MICHAEL COLLINS?
YEAH, THAT'S IT!
HIS FINGER... IT'S POINTING AT THIS SYSTEM...
SO, WHAT KIND OF MUSIC DO YOU THINK THESE GUYS LISTENED TO BACK THEN?

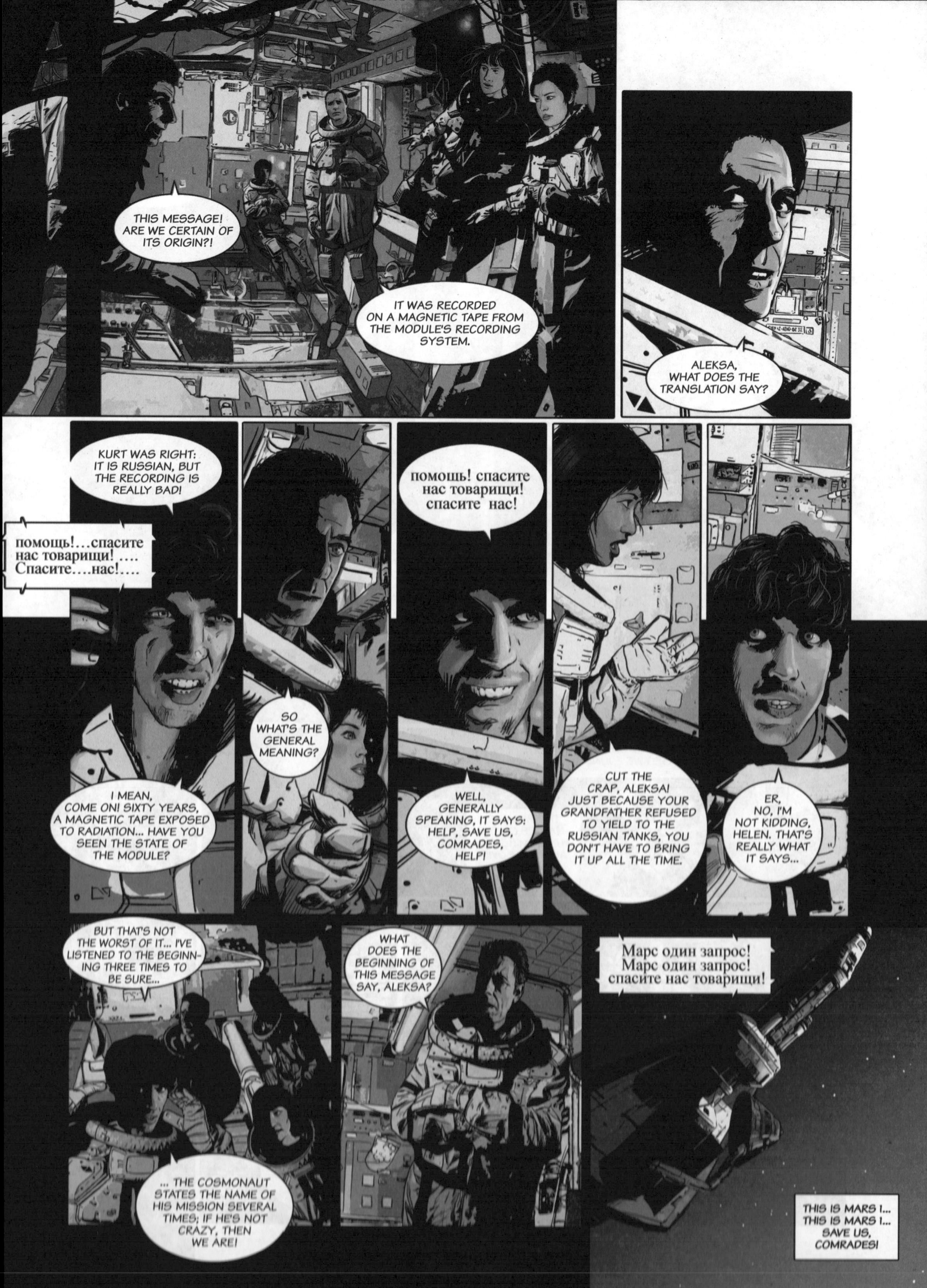

THIS MESSAGE! ARE WE CERTAIN OF ITS ORIGIN?!
IT WAS RECORDED ON A MAGNETIC TAPE FROM THE MODULE'S RECORDING SYSTEM.
ALEKSA, WHAT DOES THE TRANSLATION SAY?
помощь!…спасите нас товарищи! …. Спасите….нас!….
KURT WAS RIGHT: IT IS RUSSIAN, BUT THE RECORDING IS REALLY BAD!
I MEAN, COME ON! SIXTY YEARS, A MAGNETIC TAPE EXPOSED TO RADIATION... HAVE YOU SEEN THE STATE OF THE MODULE?
SO WHAT'S THE GENERAL MEANING?
помощь! спасите нас товарищи! спасите нас!
WELL, GENERALLY SPEAKING, IT SAYS: HELP, SAVE US, COMRADES, HELP!
CUT THE CRAP, ALEKSA! JUST BECAUSE YOUR GRANDFATHER REFUSED TO YIELD TO THE RUSSIAN TANKS, YOU DON'T HAVE TO BRING IT UP ALL THE TIME.
ER, NO, I'M NOT KIDDING, HELEN. THAT'S REALLY WHAT IT SAYS...
BUT THAT'S NOT THE WORST OF IT... I'VE LISTENED TO THE BEGINNING THREE TIMES TO BE SURE...
... THE COSMONAUT STATES THE NAME OF HIS MISSION SEVERAL TIMES; IF HE'S NOT CRAZY, THEN WE ARE!
WHAT DOES THE BEGINNING OF THIS MESSAGE SAY, ALEKSA?
Марс один запрос! Марс один запрос! спасите нас товарищи!
THIS IS MARS I... THIS IS MARS I... SAVE US, COMRADES!

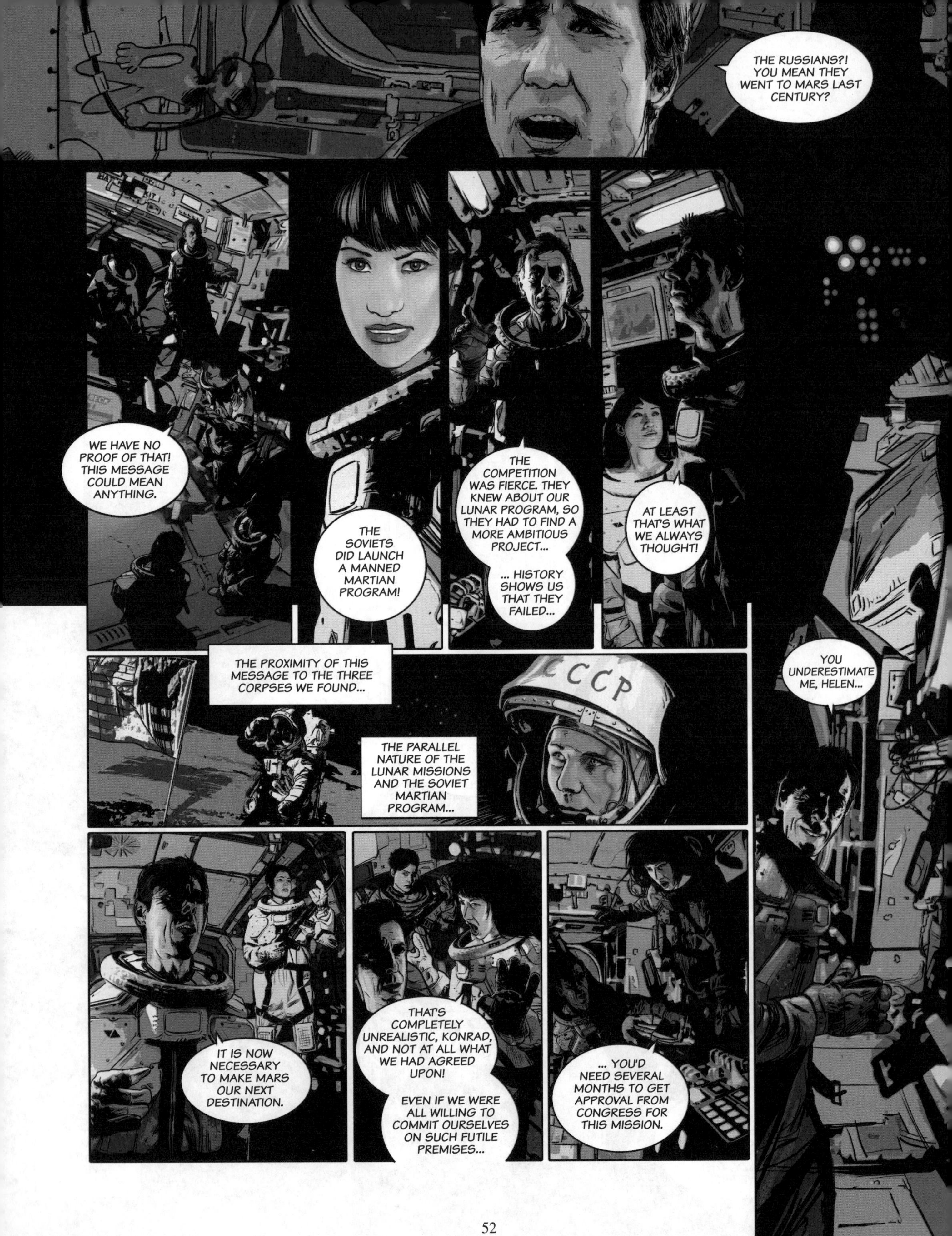

THE RUSSIANS?! YOU MEAN THEY WENT TO MARS LAST CENTURY?
WE HAVE NO PROOF OF THAT! THIS MESSAGE COULD MEAN ANYTHING.
THE SOVIETS DID LAUNCH A MANNED MARTIAN PROGRAM!
THE COMPETITION WAS FIERCE. THEY KNEW ABOUT OUR LUNAR PROGRAM, SO THEY HAD TO FIND A MORE AMBITIOUS PROJECT...
... HISTORY SHOWS US THAT THEY FAILED...
AT LEAST THAT'S WHAT WE ALWAYS THOUGHT!
THE PROXIMITY OF THIS MESSAGE TO THE THREE CORPSES WE FOUND...
CCCP
THE PARALLEL NATURE OF THE LUNAR MISSIONS AND THE SOVIET MARTIAN PROGRAM...
YOU UNDERESTIMATE ME, HELEN...
IT IS NOW NECESSARY TO MAKE MARS OUR NEXT DESTINATION.
THAT'S COMPLETELY UNREALISTIC, KONRAD, AND NOT AT ALL WHAT WE HAD AGREED UPON!
EVEN IF WE WERE ALL WILLING TO COMMIT OURSELVES ON SUCH FUTILE PREMISES...
... YOU'D NEED SEVERAL MONTHS TO GET APPROVAL FROM CONGRESS FOR THIS MISSION.

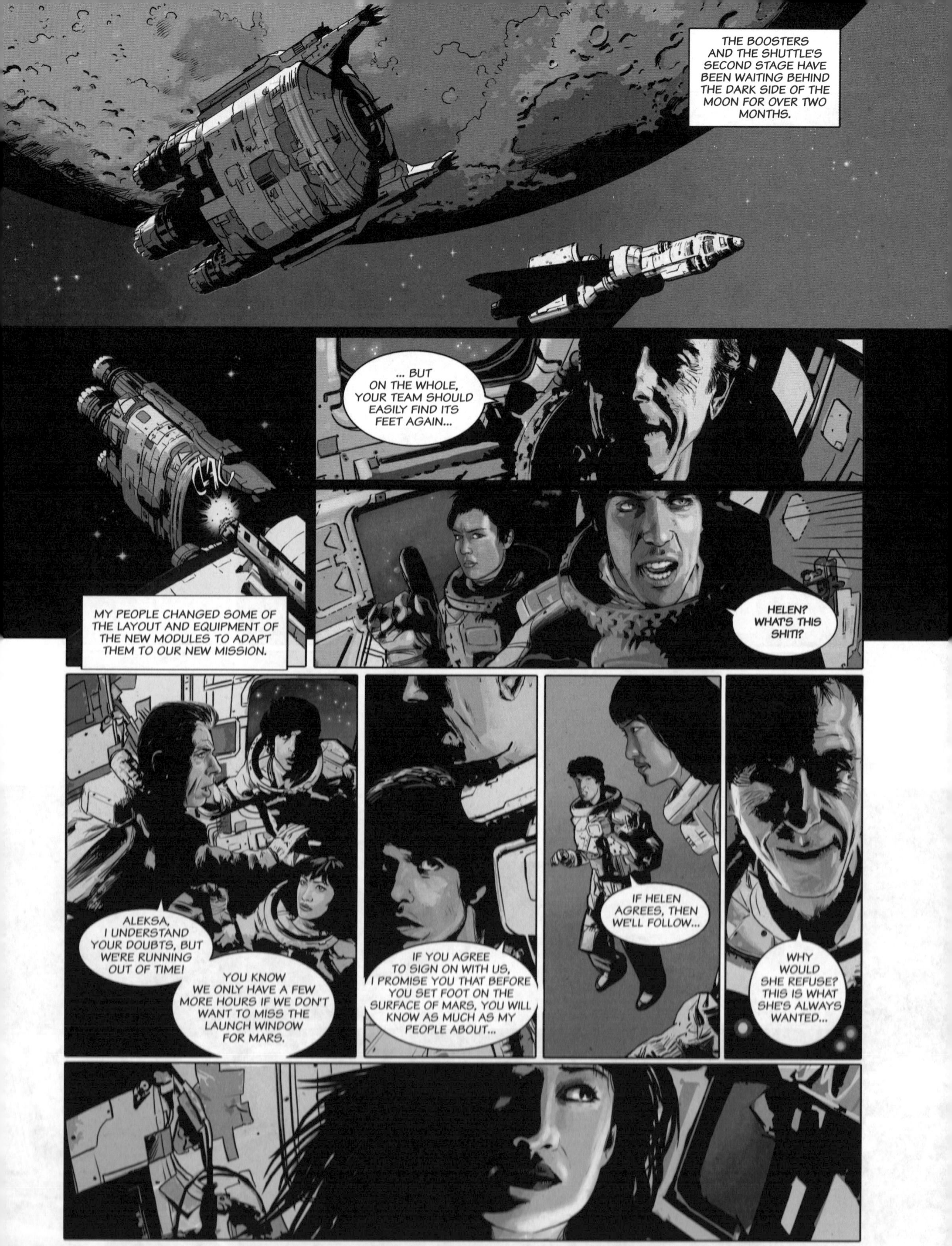
THE BOOSTERS AND THE SHUTTLE'S SECOND STAGE HAVE BEEN WAITING BEHIND THE DARK SIDE OF THE MOON FOR OVER TWO MONTHS.
... BUT ON THE WHOLE, YOUR TEAM SHOULD EASILY FIND ITS FEET AGAIN...
MY PEOPLE CHANGED SOME OF THE LAYOUT AND EQUIPMENT OF THE NEW MODULES TO ADAPT THEM TO OUR NEW MISSION.
HELEN? WHAT'S THIS SHIT!?
ALEKSA, I UNDERSTAND YOUR DOUBTS, BUT WE'RE RUNNING OUT OF TIME!
YOU KNOW WE ONLY HAVE A FEW MORE HOURS IF WE DON'T WANT TO MISS THE LAUNCH WINDOW FOR MARS.
IF YOU AGREE TO SIGN ON WITH US, I PROMISE YOU THAT BEFORE YOU SET FOOT ON THE SURFACE OF MARS, YOU WILL KNOW AS MUCH AS MY PEOPLE ABOUT...
IF HELEN AGREES, THEN WE'LL FOLLOW...
WHY WOULD SHE REFUSE? THIS IS WHAT SHE'S ALWAYS WANTED...

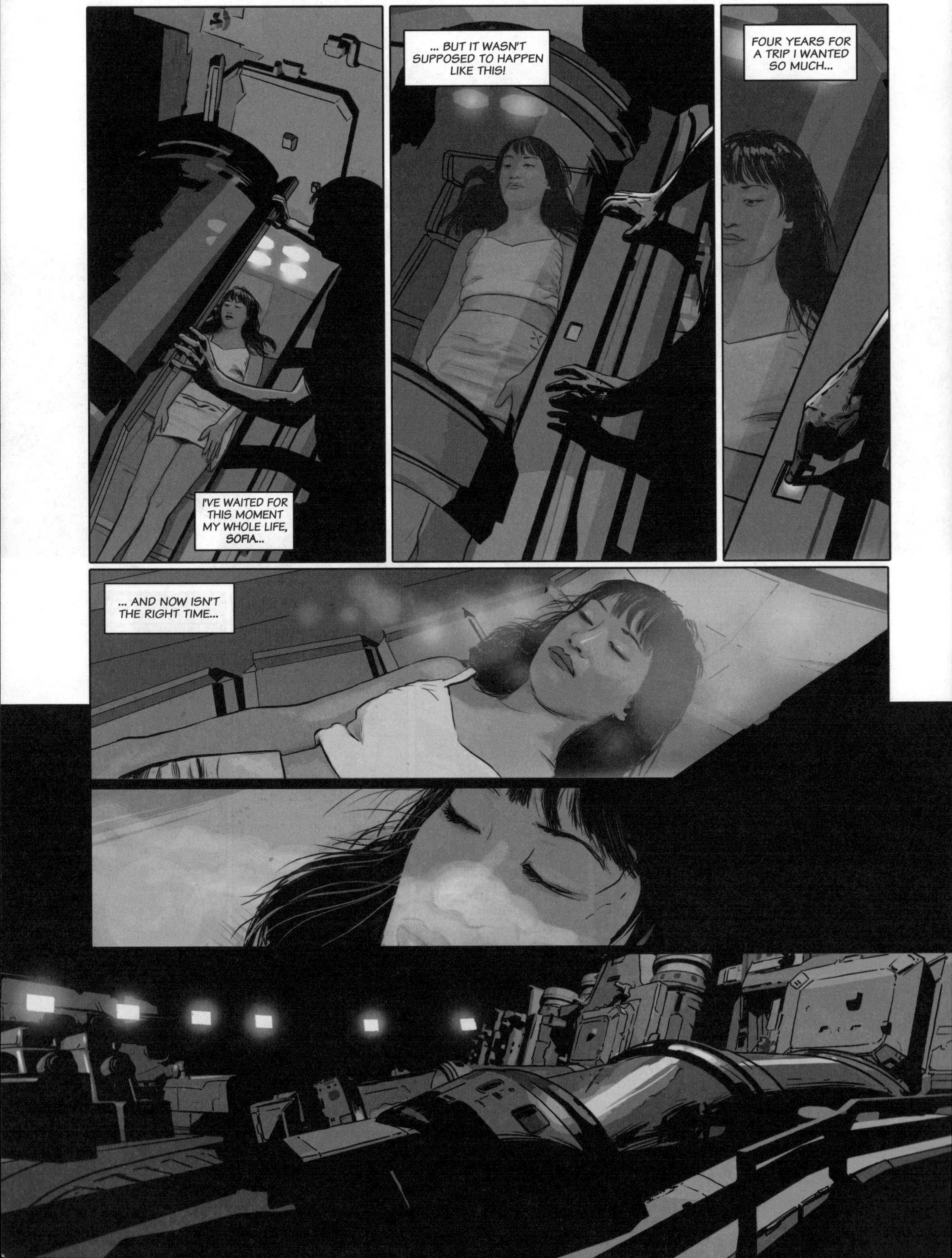
I'VE WAITED FOR THIS MOMENT MY WHOLE LIFE, SOFIA...
... BUT IT WASN'T SUPPOSED TO HAPPEN LIKE THIS!
FOUR YEARS FOR A TRIP I WANTED SO MUCH...
... AND NOW ISN'T THE RIGHT TIME...

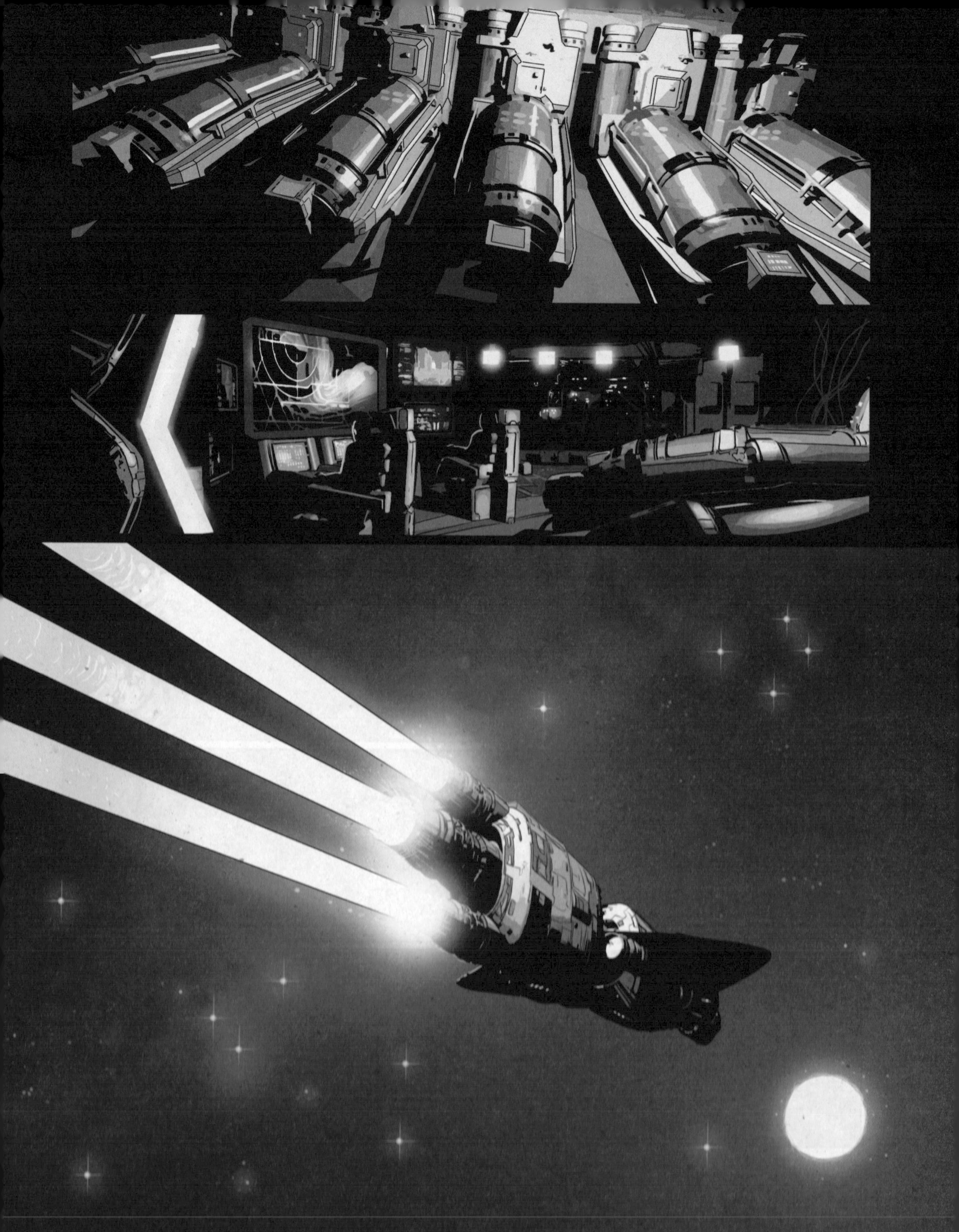

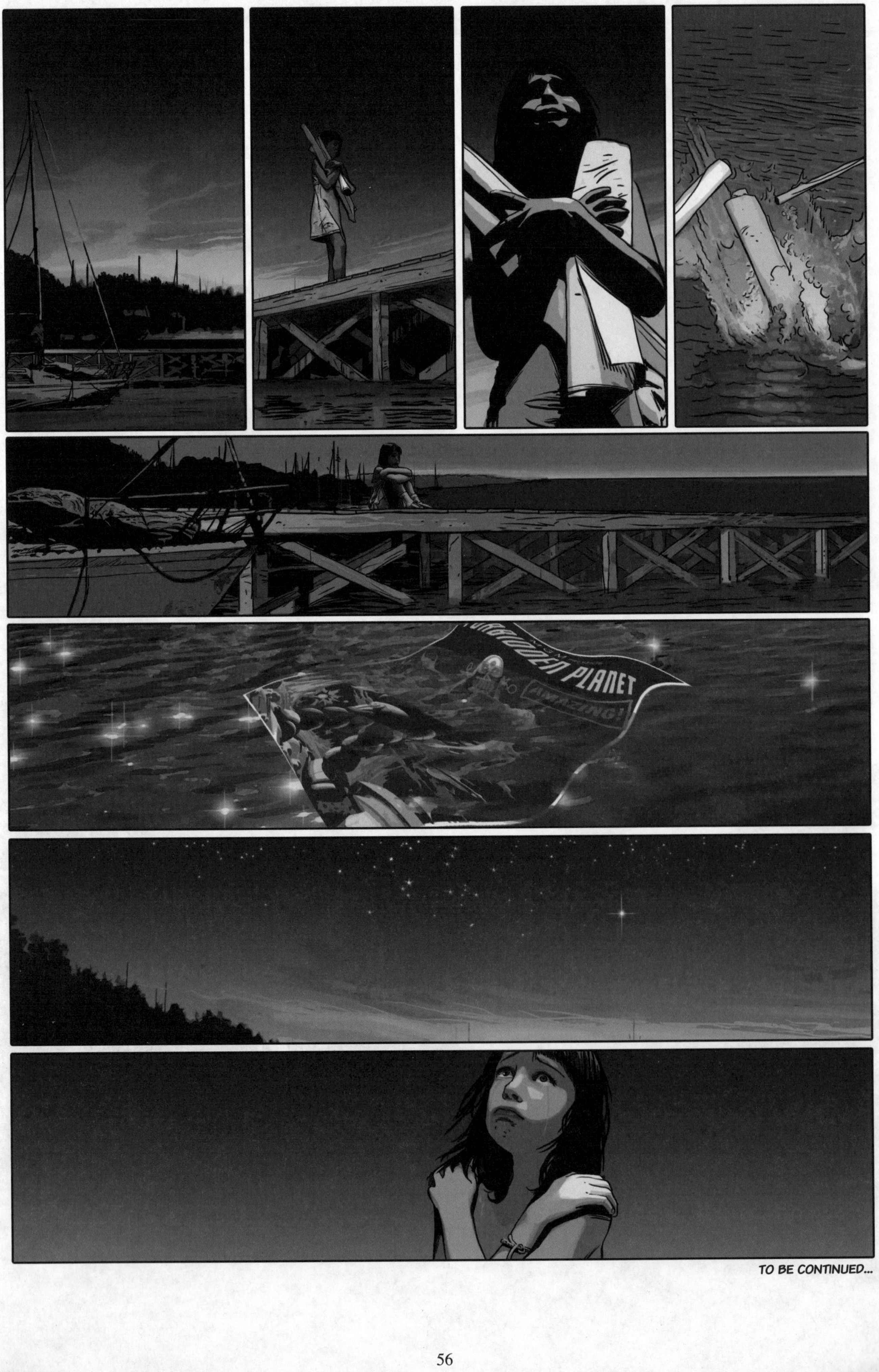
PLANET
AMAZING!

TO BE CONTINUED...